H.R.F. KEATING
Jack the LADY KILLER

POISONED PEN PRESS

M

First published in Great Britain in 1999 by Flambard Press
Stable Cottage, East Fourstones, Hexham NE47 5DX

First U.S. Edition, 1999 Poisoned Pen Press

Typeset by Barbara Sumner
Cover design by Gainford Design Associates
Author photograph by Simon Keating
Printed by Cromwell Press, Trowbridge, Wiltshire

The picture on the front cover, 'Tiger Hunt',
is reproduced by permission of the V&A Picture Gallery.

The decorative tailpieces are from Captain Mundy's *Pen
and Pencil Sketches, Being the Journal of A Tour in India*.

A CIP catalogue record for this book
is available from the British Library.

ISBN 1-890208-24-8
Library of Congress Card Catalog Number: 99-66272

© 1999 H.R.F. Keating

Poisoned Pen Press
6962 E. 1st. Ave. #103
Scottsdale, AZ 85251
www.poisonedpenpress.com

PREFACE

The novel in verse is a rare form today, for the sufficient reason that readers are dead scared of it. Vikram Seth in his splendid verse portrait of pleasure-seeking life in San Francisco, *The Golden Gate*, has a few lines which put this delightfully neatly:

> An editor – at a plush party
> … seized my arm: 'Dear fellow,
> What's your next work?' 'A novel…' 'Great!
> We hope that you, dear Mr. Seth –'
> 'In verse,' I added. He turned yellow.
> 'How marvellously quaint,' he said,
> And subsequently cut me dead.

But, in fact, *The Golden Gate* triumphantly proves what a good form the verse novel is, especially when it employs the strict formal pattern Mr Seth uses, taken from Charles Johnston's excellent translation of Pushkin's great narrative poem *Eugene Onegin*. In turn, *The Golden Gate* made me think: 'If he can do it as a novel, couldn't I possibly do it as a crime novel?'

However, when it came to it, though I was able to get some of the on-rushing readability Vikram Seth achieved by employing his short lines, I was too unskilled to emulate completely his alternating masculine and feminine rhymes. Nonetheless I discovered, as I guess he too did, that paradoxically the difficulty of expressing one's thoughts in the apparently restrictive rhyme-form we have both adopted allows one to say extra things which might never have risen from the subconscious if one were writing straightforward prose. The rhyme pattern, too, curiously enough, helps, more or less unconsciously, to speed a reader onwards. So plunge on to the roller-coaster and let it happen to you.

Jack, the Lady Killer is, in fact, not quite the first crime novel in poetic form. Some two years ago, when I had completed my first draft, I came across in a bookshop a novel of crime in the form of a series of poems, short and longer, in *vers libre*. This was *The Monkey's Mask*, an erotic murder mystery by the Australian poet Dorothy Porter, who has also written an historical novel in verse. But how does it come about that my draft was ready that long ago? Simple. Publishers are as stiffly reluctant as readers to trust themselves to the helter-skelter. It is due only to the bravery of Peter and Margaret Lewis of the Flambard Press in England and of Barbara Peters and Robert Rosenwald at their American co-publishers, the Poisoned Pen Press, that *Jack* is in your hands now.

Vikram Seth, that most versatile of writers, followed *The Golden Gate* with a very long novel (in prose), set in his native India, *A Suitable Boy*, again wonderful. I did not try to follow him quite like that. Since composing *Jack* I have written two novels also set in India, of which I am distinctly not a native but, I like to think, an honorary citizen. The second of these is only just finished (and so without a final title). The first was the twentieth outing for Inspector Ghote of the Bombay C.I.D., or now of the Mumbai C.I.D. He began his career in 1964, and has been kind enough to provide me with two Gold Dagger awards, from the British Crime Writers' Association. But, more importantly, seeing life through his eyes has enabled me, by contrasting Indian ways with Western, to bring to the fore the common aspects of our humanity and perhaps to look at them a little more deeply. Much the same thing occurs, I feel, in contrasting, not Indian and Western ways, but the habits of thought in India in the 1930s and our habits of thought today. I hope my readers will find that stimulating.

H.R.F. KEATING
London, June 1999

'The old folks settle down with books:
He with *Tom Jones*, she with a thriller
Entitled *Jack the Lady-Killer*.'
Vikram Seth, *The Golden Gate*

PROLOGUE

Jack, the Lady Killer, there's
my title, chosen for this tale.
A tribute, bold, from one who dares
follow a poet (will I fail?)
of sparkling wit and dazzling rhyme.
But, as for me, I'll stick to crime.
Vikram Seth's *The Golden Gate*,
my quote's from that. If not quite straight,
it holds my plot in embryo.
But where to set my nascent verse?
Answer: yes, I can't do worse
than India. So, there I'll go,
back to my old stamping ground.
But with a yesteryear sleuthhound.

THE PEOPLE OF THE POEM

Little Brown Gramophone: A small Indian boy, a *chhokra*, with a curious gift. Could he be our hero?

Jack Steele: A rather bigger English lad, a new recruit to the Imperial Police Service in India. Could *he* be our hero?

F.H.R. Guthrie: District Superintendent of Police. He would, if he knew he was in a story, be certain he was its hero.

Edward Carter: A planter. Flashy enough to be a hero, only he hides his light under a bushel.

Dr Prosser: Civil Surgeon at the Station. Fat, fussy and, to tell the truth, usually drunk. No sort of hero.

Bulaki Ram: A police sergeant or *havildar*. If in the days of the British Raj an Indian could be in any way a hero, he would qualify.

Milly Marchbanks: Widow of the former Club secretary. Only if a woman man-eater could be a hero would she be.

Matron: In charge of nursing at the Station hospital. An heroically sturdy lady.

The Rev. Peter Fox: The Padre, the Station chaplain. Expected to be heroically saintly, of course.

Arthur Brent: A Government engineer. An unsung hero of the Raj.

Miss Jacqueline Browne: Club domestic supervisor. Another one with a light under a bushel. An heroic light?

'Plum' Duff: An old India hand, now Club secretary. The least heroic of all figures.

District Commissioner Derek Wright: Figure of authority. A statutory hero in every white man's eyes.

Mrs Wright: Derek Wright's wife. To her he is no hero.

Mr Corbyn: A Member of Parliament on a fact-finding mission. Too little of a hero to find even one buried fact.

Jessica Corbyn: His niece, who may or may not see Jack Steele as her hero.

PART ONE

The place? Punjab, its dusty plains.
The time our story comes alive?
A time gone by, a day's remains,
India, 1935.
Our hero? He's a lad called Jack.
Just that. Not John. Alas, alack,
that single name will be a weight
around his neck, a heavy fate.
Before we reach our final word
he'll curse this name that is his own.
A name, he thinks, not his alone
but a killer's, though unheard.
A killer Jack – it's much to ask –
will find his duty to unmask.

Jack Steele, an innocent abroad, arrives in the India of the British Raj.

But there's another boy who'll play
a major part in this our tale.
A very different lad. Let's say
a pole apart. Yes, he's male,
but that is all that links the two.
Our Jack is one who's going to
rule the land where he's arrived.
The other's one who hasn't thrived
in any way, not half Jack's age,
an orphan kid with just one gift,
one talent, one, that just will lift
the little boy on to our page.
But there he'll have a major part.
You'll find him at the story's heart.

'Little Brown Gramophone',
that's what he's called by one and all.
All hangs on him, on him alone,
upon his gift, however small.
It is a trick he's always had,
the mimic's gift for good or bad.
Yes, bad or good, the fact remains:
words heard just once he then retains,
whether in English or Punjabi,
or even both together blended.
Quite often scarcely comprehended
(the sahib's shout 'Bring whisky *pani*'),
whatever words this *chhokra* heard
he'd parrot back, the boy a bird.

And that is all the worldly wealth
the boy, aged eight, or nine, or seven,
has to his name. Not cash, nor health
(already a cough's predicting heaven,
or, as a Hindu, one more life).
His gift, then, perched upon a knife-
edge. But his gift's the single clue
to the black puzzle shortly due
to confront our hero, Jack.
And Jack, be sure, is still unskilled
(it's not enough just to have willed)
in sahibdom, still to learn the knack
of ruling a whole sub-continent
by guile, by force, by sentiment.

For these three strains in far-off days
combined in India to uphold
a master race. The steady gaze
of just one man, unbending, bold,
would quail a thousand, kind yet stern.
This gaze Jack Steele has still to learn,
just six months here. A mere nineteen,
he must not think what he has been,
a boy immured at boarding school.
Oh yes, he was a leader then,
yet those he led were scarcely men.
But now he's being trained to rule,
to act the sahib, to be a god,
nor fear, nor favour. Wield the rod.

And who's he got as trainer guide?
A sahib of sahibs, a gentleman,
an India hand in wool deep-dyed,
the sahibest sahib in all the clan.
Yes, though young Jack is quite at sea,
he is not left to wander free.
No, India's Imperial Police,
keeper of King-Emperor's peace,
provides as shepherd, ward and watch,
one Mr Guthrie, 'F.H.R.'
or 'R.H.F.' or 'H.F.R.'
By those initials (placed hotch-potch
as often as the right way round)
he's called by all. And he is sound.

So watch Jack as he bells the cat.
Let's eavesdrop on the master's teaching,
which Guthrie Sahib describes as 'chat'.
Teaching? Well, perhaps it's preaching.
So, see him there spoonfeeding Jack,
pipe in mouth, chair tilted back.
A man of forty, not much more,
blue-eyed, lean, hard to the core,
red-armed, red-legged, in shorts and shirt,
thick yellow hair on both, a pelt.
Across his chest his Sam Browne belt.
And nowhere any spot of dirt.
That's Guthrie Sahib, called F.H.R.,
who prides himself on seeing far.

We've found them in the police *daftar*,
Jack newly here, no lessons read,
now learning not from his Papa
but from this quasi-Dad instead.
Guthrie's now *parentis loco*,
saying what's 'done' and what is no go.
'You've been out riding? Excellent, lad.
Keep fit, keep fit. Or you'll go bad.
By saying *bad* don't think I mean
you'll lose your tone, or lose your zest.
I mean that soon – don't think I jest –
you'll take to drink, or find you've been
eyeing black bints with evil thoughts.
Worse, letting John T. escape your shorts.

Talking of that, of, you know, sex,
don't think that every lady here
– just as well to clear the decks –
always wears, well, her underwear.
Most, of course, are pukka mems,
jewels in the Crown, just perfect gems.
But, listen, lad, yet don't repeat it,
if Milly beckons, smile – and beat it.
Milly Marchbanks, widow lady,
should have gone Home when old Mike died.
But you be warned: she's pretty shady,
a shady lady, now untied
from marriage bonds, if ever heeded.
Ask me, lad, a spanking's needed.'

Guthrie stops short. He's said too much.
He coughs, looks down, picks up a file.
'Excuse me, lad, if like a Dutch
uncle I go on.' A smile.
'But I'll be frank. There was last year
a boy like you and stationed here,
not in the Police, but Forestry.
And into Milly's claws, well, he
fell. Or jumped. I don't know which.
Milly the Man-eater, her claws are hid,
but eat that boy was what she did.
A suicide. Hushed up. The bitch
still lives, with no regrets. That's her.
I could say more, but – but, well, – er …

Word to the wise, eh, my son John?
'nough said. Now, first things first.
Your topee. Out-of-doors without that on –
and sunstroke. Yes, with that we're cursed.
Of course, the natives never wear them,
or just a cloth. But the sun don't scare 'em.
They're different from us. Remember, Jack:
we are White and they are Black.'
'Yes, sir. But – Well ...' 'Come, spit it out.'
'Well, back Home some that I met
seemed decent sorts.' 'Oh, yes, I bet
that's what they seemed. But, make no doubt,
there underneath they, every one,
of your kind heart were making fun.'

Jack Steele feels now it's time to go.
He's on the point of leaving, but –
'Just one thing more you need to know:
bowels open, lad, and mouth kept shut.
Remember: natives everywhere.
Watch p's and q's, and be aware.
You're on show, lad, from dawn till dusk.
Yes. Look at that, that mounted tusk.
I shot that beast. Do you know why?
A crowd of natives waited there
to see if I would funk the dare.
They waited just to see if I
lacked the guts to kneel and shoot.
No other course: I killed the brute.'

Outside, Jack stands, topee askew.
He needs some time for solid thought.
What Guthrie's told him's hardly new
– it's new in detail, not import.
From his earliest days at school
he knew that Britain's there to rule.
He knew, as true, that ones like one
are there to say what's to be done.
The Empire, let no foe defile.
The Union Jack, the red-marked map,
a task God gave to every chap
born within the sacred isle.
But till this moment he had not
wholly realised where he'd got.

To India. Where the schoolboy Jack
is all at once more than a man.
The Empire's weight is on my back.   His feeling of
Now I am my country's spokesman.   dread at the
Yes, all of that and even more.   role he has
(Jack shifts, as if his shoulder's sore.)   to shoulder.
Prestige is what I must uphold.
Without that life's just 'bought and sold'.
Now every day – it's Empire's gift –
I must live life up to that mark
whether in sun or in night's dark.
Never to know the burden lift.
He feels oppressed, a pinning weight.
Lifts hands to put his topee straight.

And what has placed the burden there?
Fifteen years of reading stories.
Tales and texts in classrooms where
they spoke of all the Empire's glories.
Kipling, held up as fixed in marble,
then Henty's *With Roberts to Kabul*,
a hundred yarns of derring-do,
Ballantyne, Stevenson, the whole crew.
And music, Elgar's martial thumping
(plus England's countryside evoked.
'None of your Germans,' Dad had joked.)
Accounts of loyal natives humping
in some brave explorer's wake,
striding out for Britain's sake.

Move on. Move on some months or more.   Finding his
And we now see a tennis court   feet, he does
where Jack's in play, not quite so raw.   well in the
The Club is where this battle's fought.   Club tennis
The Club, the hub of British life.   tournament.
For every Briton, man and wife,
it is their centre, safe, secure,
where talk's unbuttoned, sport is pure.
The tournament, the year's highlight,
is taking place as it has done
year after year since 1901.
The winner's Cup is shining bright.
'Guthrie', its last two shields proclaim.
Victory today will seal his fame.

But Jack's the one who now is playing
his *Burra Sahib*. The semi-final.
And to him it's most dismaying
(he'd love to hide in the urinal).
Because, thanks to his well-honed skill,
he's ended here, against his will,
on pretty sharp dilemma horns.
To lose on purpose? Or tread corns
by playing well and, most like, winning?
Knock out his boss? He thinks he could
(the fact is that he's very good)
but Guthrie Sahib, he knows, is pinning
all his hopes on this last chance.
At his back the years advance.

The Cup, or 'pot' as Guthrie dubs it,
– but Jack has glimpsed, a daunting sight,
Guthrie yearning as he rubs it –
means for him Time's speeding flight.
So (Jack thinks) should I now quit?
Lose, though make a fight of it?
Then the man who is my chief
can feel, yes, still, he is Time's thief.
But if I play as I was taught,
play up, play up and play the game,
I'll put my boss to inner shame.
No, though I know well what I ought
to do, I won't. I'll let him win.
Losing, is it such a sin?

First set, Guthrie. Score: 6–4.
The second's Jack's, a quick 6–2.
Now the decider. Ten games more,
Jack thinks. Lose six, win four. Then who
tomorrow? Yes, just Edward Carter.
He'll play the Final. I'll be a martyr.
Carter's quite good but much too flash,
the sort that F.H.R. could thrash
with one hand tied behind his back.
But Guthrie seems to lose his fire.
Several of his serves are dire.
So is he tiring, wonders Jack.
And if he is, how can I lose?
He racks his brains for some excuse.

Then Guthrie serves a double fault,
and misses next an easy hit.
But now the Umpire calls a halt.
A servant has brought out a chit.
The Umpire – it is Dr Prosser –
reads, then calls across a
puzzled Guthrie, who in turn
reads and frowns. 'No, don't adjourn,'
he's heard to say, and back he comes
to face Jack's serve, which he gets back.
He seems in better form, thinks Jack.
But, no. Again he soon succumbs
to Jack's assault. Now, here's the catch.
Ten minutes more, he's lost the match.

Yet Guthrie takes defeat with grace,
an Englishman seen at his best.
'Can't win 'em all, old chap. The race
to the strong. Now, be my guest.
A *burra peg*? You've earned a drink.'
Jack does not know quite what to think.
He has a sort of under-sense
that this is false. The man's too tense.
How did he come to lose the match?
And now without another word
he's gone. Off like a shot. Absurd.
Absurd. Yet where's the catch?
I thought he'd stay a bit and chat.
Why has he just gone off like that?

And then a thought: at just past noon
when at the Club all were asleep
(and those at home, this is a boon,
the midday snooze, oblivion deep)
Jack with his boss was hard at work.
'Lad,' Guthrie'd said, 'I never shirk
when duty calls, and you should not.'
(Yet Jack once saw him rub that 'pot'.)
Report came in at the *daftar*
an elephant had snapped its chain
(a beast in *musth* one must restrain),
a rumour rumbling from afar.
And Guthrie'd said, 'I hate to kill,
but if I must, well then, I will.'

He remembers
a talk with
Guthrie a few
hours earlier.

Jack thought it all was bazaar *gup*.
But say it's true? Had Guthrie heard?
The chit that servant boy brought up?
A beast to shoot? And he deterred?
Yes, only earlier today
I learnt that killing's not his way.
That's something I can feel for, too.
It's not a thing I'd like to do.
All right, when once a beast's gone wild
you have to stop it. That's the rule.
But – this I even learnt at school,
I'd read it even as a child –
not every elephant stays mad.
The *musth* goes off, however bad.

A single shot, if it's done right,
four tons of life just blown out.
And – let the thought peep out to light –
it's dangerous, too. Have any doubt
of when to fire or where to aim
and then you learn: big game's no game.
A wounded beast will tread you down,
shake you to death, a sawdust clown.
No wonder Guthrie went off form
thinking of that, and how before
he'd faced that task, obeyed the law
of British grit, the White Man's norm.
While on the court, as shots were clapped,
he'd think: once more they've got me trapped.

They've got me trapped. But who those *they*?
The natives watching for a fall?
Or Britons braying 'British way'?
Jack shakes his head. That's not at all
what he should think. Back Home perhaps
thinking that would be no lapse,
but here beneath the Indian sun
it's one for all, and all for one.
Another drink? No. Whisky's out.
That way, he warned me, trouble lies.
A *nimbu pani* will suffice.
Soda and lime, and damn all doubt.
Jack sips, accepts congratulations,
and smiles away felicitations.

An hour goes by. The drink flows free.
'Another one?' 'Well, down the hatch.'
'Will Steele J beat Carter E?'
The talk is of tomorrow's match.
No word that Guthrie's not a sport,
but Jack wonders if the thought
is here and there allowed to rise.
His disappearance caused surprise.
But all the while a crisis hides.
Do not forget young Gramophone.
He's waiting there, as yet unknown.
Laugh, Jack, and joke. Your fate abides.
That other *chhokra's* time is near.
His hour will come. Its footfalls hear.

PART TWO

'Guthrie Sahib, come quick, come quick!'   His fate? To
A sergeant bursts in on the scene.   shoot an
'Steady now. Is this some trick?'   elephant? Or
the Doctor, swift to intervene.   one yet darker?
'*Hathi* has killed. The D.S.P.
must come. Please, Daktar, vere is he?'
They send the servants everywhere.
Guthrie not found, not far nor near.
So now all eyes swing round to Jack.
An elephant that has gone mad.
Here's a task for the new-come lad.
Jack tries a grin. 'I'll have a crack.'
A beast to shoot, all seem to say
Jack Steele this is your lucky day.

And hardly any time goes by,
it seems to Jack, before he finds
himself all set. But why, oh, why,   He rides off
he asks in secret. In two minds.   to do his
One half is thinking *This is it,*   duty, however
my chance to show I'll do my bit.   dangerous.
But, as his pony trots, another
voice inside, one hard to smother,
asks why. Why should I shoot
an animal that – who's to say? –
may be a killer or it may
be rumour's victim, not a brute.
And, more, to someone it's his wealth.
It's food, it's land, it's shelter, health.

The elephant, Jack's slow to reason,
is in a way what we are here for.
It's India. To kill one, treason.
Surely we, the British, therefore
should nurture them and only when
no other course exists, well, then
with fire we should fight fire.
If thus with beasts that we admire,
so should it be with humankind.
We should be here to lead and aid.
Yes, once, through blood we had to wade.
The Mutiny brought bloodshed blind.
But nowadays we should preserve
the good. Then good in turn deserve.

But all too soon the time has gone
for questioning why this, why that.
Jack spots a crowd, and further on ...
Now *Now might I do it pat.*
Prince Hamlet's words seem all too apt.
Like Hamlet, am I conscience trapped?
No murdering King for me to kill.
But, yes, royal beast for good or ill.
There a hundred yards away
it stands. And tranquil as can be,
eating with frankly joyous glee
trunk-loads of grass. No beast at bay,
but centrepiece of some quiet scene.
A pastoral of what has been.

Jack halts, and then uncertainly
speaks to those just standing there
and asks, in halting Punjabi,
if truly it is cause for fear.
'Oh, sahib,' an answer quickly came,
'let it live now, it is your shame.
That beast, once quiet, has killed today.
One poor man got in its way.'
A dozen more their stories retail.
A life for a life is all the shout.
But underneath Jack scents a doubt.
Those stories lack convincing detail.
So still he seeks for some delay,
wishes that Guthrie were not away.

Yet he's been hunted high and low,
and no one's found his dour retreat,
a hideyhole where he can go
to nurse the smart of his defeat.
But, Jack thinks, if only now he'd
just appear and do this deed
that I must do, or so it seems.
A nightmare. Yes, the worst of dreams.
I feel like one who's faced with two
tasks he's pledged to, neither one
that's right or wrong. To take my gun
and shoot to kill a creature who
looks a picture of pure calm?
Or to fail to blot out harm?

Then, too, this crowd's just seeking fun
or even, those who touch it, meat,
those tons of flesh that when my gun
brings them to earth are theirs to eat.
No. No, I will not shoot that beast.
Or I'll wait until at least
it's certain that it killed that man.
Rumour here, I know well, can
flare up from nothing like a match
put to a heap of twigs or straw,
and in a minute, scarcely more,
the flames are licking out to catch
a village in their greedy claws,
leaping onwards without pause.

But, wait, there is another thing
that ought – ought it? – to make me act.
There's prestige. Britain's. The King-
Emperor, no less, is to be backed
in even such a small event
as this. Because the littlest dent
in British majesty and pride
can leave a trough, deep, yes, and wide.
Black hearts are waiting then to pour
through in one sharp-mocking sea.
That's what I've had drummed into me.
Am I to break that laid-down law?
Below, the elephant he sees
cleaning its grass against its knees.

So, now cram feeling down. Jack knew,
for all the elephant should live,
that what it was he had to do
was what he'd do. Poor brute, forgive:
one moment he allowed that thought.
Some lessons there are dearly bought,
but his he thinks that he has learnt.
The fire he fears: the child's been burnt.
So solemnly he loads his gun.
Four cartridges he slips in place,
and then a fifth one just in case.
The watching crowd, for them it's fun,
he thinks. For me perhaps my death.
Two minutes more, and my last breath.

And still the seekers after fun
are watching, all with avid eyes.
So what's to do must now be done.
I am afraid, but must disguise
the smallest hint of craven fear.
Now, walk on down until I'm near
enough to hit the single spot,
they say, is where to put your shot.
Five paces. Ten. Another ten.
Then on one knee and take cool aim.
Miss that one spot, you only maim,
enrage the beast. And it's death then.
But, God, it looks so tranquil there.
Deep breath, keep still, don't move a hair.

Jack hardly feels the gun's recoil,
and there below all's as before.
Nothing. No drama, no turmoil.
A minute seems to pass, or more.
But then a jerk in those thick knees.
Jack sees the life-blood slow, then cease.
Two thoughts at once are in his head:
One shot, I did it and *Would I were dead.*
What is this thing that I have done?
Committed murder. Yes, it's that.
But who'll arrest this murdering rat?
No one. Not anyone at all. This gun
won't be tagged on the evidence table.
No. *Hero*: that'll be my label.

And so it was, back at the Club.
The tale was told, the single shot.
One minute's work. And then the cub
was turned into a man, if not
more than a man, a superman.
Though Jack suspected that his span
would not be long in such a role.
The stallion shortly back to foal.
Yet he was wrong, as it turned out.
Ten minutes more and – twice it's been –
the sergeant burst in on the scene.
Now, once again, there came his shout.
'Steele Sahib, Steele Sahib, please to come quick.
Sahib, a murder. Sahib, no trick.'

For just an instant Jack's head reels.   Now his
This is what happened hours ago.   testing hour
Consternation's all he feels.   has come with
It happened when I had to go,   a vengeance.
to face the elephant I shot.
Has time reversed? What's happened? What?
But then the word the sergeant yelled
sinks in. *Murder*. Its echo swelled
and swelled and swelled. Jack frowned.
Murder. But who? And where? And why?
And, once again, it seems that I
am called upon. Guthrie found?
No. Or they'd not ask for me.
But Guthrie? Guthrie, where is he?

In his confusion Jack had spoken
half-aloud, though quite in vain.
But outside, the spell now broken,
he asked his question once again.
'Sahib,' the sergeant then replied,
'D.S.P. has almost died.'   He is told
'Died? How? Why? He wasn't ill.'   why his chief,
'Sahib, they found him on the hill.   the District
Sun had touched him on his head.'   Superintendent
'So where's he now?' 'Sahib, most sick   of Police,
in hop'ital. But, sahib, come quick.   vanished.
Marchbanks Memsahib she is dead.'
'Dead? And murdered, did you say?'
'*Jee*, sahib, it has to be that vay.'

'But why? What's this? Where – where is she?'
'Strangled, sahib, beside her bed.'
'I'll come at once. But – when was she –'
'Sahib, all afternoon she's dead.'
'Who was it found her body then?'
'Not found, sahib. Sir, it was ven
ek native heard.' 'Heard? Heard what?
Strangled, you said, so not a shot.'
'No, sir, it was vords she shouted.
Sir, she shouted *No, Jack, no!*'
'Who heard her then? And did they go
and see who ...' Jack doubted
if all this was true. It seemed
like something he had dreamed.

A moment later light was thrown.
'Sahib, it was the boy who heard.
Sahib, Little Brown Gramophone.'
'What? That boy who – That's absurd.'
'Sahib, no. He is playing near
ven that shout come in his ear.
And, sahib, you know all he is hearing
he would repeat. Song or swearing
in Punjabi, English. Or some bird
just only singing, even a cart
go squeaking by. Or, sahib, a fart.'
Jack frowns. 'Sahib, please, is not absurd.'
But Jack feels now he's sharply pricked.
No native should dare contradict.

But, no. This fellow's right. I'm wrong.
Jack's quick to cancel what he'd thought.
That boy repeats both word and song.
Tell no lies, you're not in court.
That saying's true about the kid.
He cannot lie. He never did.
He is, in truth, a gramophone.
Why, once some words of mine came back,
each syllable exactly so,
I thought *My double's speaking here.*
Like microphones each little ear.
So if a cry of *No, Jack, no!*
came to those ears, then it shrilled out.
Of that there cannot be a doubt.

And now Jack's at the murder scene,   His chief out
Marchbanks Sahib's old bungalow.   of action,
Close to the Club, it's always been,   he goes
since distant ages long ago,   to inspect
the perquisite of the Hon. Sec.   the corpse.
Jack enters. And it is a wreck.
It looks as if, to Jack's wide eyes,
a gale's swept through, of ultra-size.
Chairs, tables, cards, a torn page
from some flung book – all its state
is evidence of how her fate
arose from some wild burst of rage.
Jack thinks: What's done and can't be mended,
a life – a card game – sharply ended.

And then, the corpse. Yes, death is real.
Jack's never yet seen someone dead,
or not close to. What should I feel,
he asks himself across the bed
where Milly lies, a tossed-down sprawl.
What do I feel? Just *Is this all?*
One woman's life the sum of years
reduced to this. Not Fate's fell shears,
but ugly marks around the neck.
A body looking like a doll,
and, yes, the reek of alcohol.
Once a woman, now a wreck.
But someone brought this void about.
Mine the task to find them out.

Jack looks and looks. But not a sign
of anything to tell him who
or how, what sort of swine
rampaged like that. No, not a clue
to show me how this came about.
Oh God, he thinks, I'm quite without
a single hint. And then it comes.
Yes, I have one. A thought that numbs.
Yes. *Jack.* The name the boy repeated.
The killer, then, must be called Jack.
So, God, it's not some dacoit pack
of raping natives in lust heated.
Or thieves come swooping like a kite.
Jack. No, the murderer must be white.

But if the killer's one of us   <small>The murderer</small>
it's clear that here's a matter that   <small>proved to be</small>
I must try never to discuss   <small>a sahib, he</small>
with anyone. *Under my hat*   <small>feels he can</small>
my motto now. However much   <small>trust no one.</small>
I yearn for prop, I yearn for crutch.
All alone I'll have to find
this Jack and what he hides behind.
So now, a mental note. Yes, I
must stop the *chhokra* from repeating
under threat of a sound beating
to any soul his *No, Jack!* cry.
I trust, he adds, a threat's enough,
but come what may I must be tough.

So now he thinks of all he knows
about the victim and her ways.
He knows a lot. Under the rose
(as they say) he's learnt that days
and days go by and no one sees
Milly. Or bar some buck, and he's
seeing her at dead of night.
Her bungalow is shut up tight,
and there inside she sits with cards
in front of her, a Patience game.
Day after day it is the same.
Her widowed privacy she guards
from all save those she seeks to eat.
By night man-eater takes her meat.

One other thing Jack finds he knows.
Man-eater, just like any lion,
in lioness rage will turn on those
she's loved and lost like red-hot iron.
Others have whispered sotto voce,
words tear-stained and voice blotchy,
what he had heard at least in hint
from F.H.R. He's eyed a-squint
those who told him; but he's heard.
Yes, he thinks, not all around
feel like Guthrie duty-bound
to silence. No, *a dicky-bird,*
they're apt to say, *told me all,*
and listen ... goes the gossips' drawl.

Another thought. A creeping fear
slides in. It's this: just how can I
speak of this to that man here
who's seen and knows? He's like a spy
on every English weakness and
on worse. Guthrie made me understand
that much when first I set foot here.
Oh, F.H.R., why are you there
in hospital when I need you?
If you were fit all this would rest
on you, and I'd not face this test.
You'd have seen, I'm sure, the clue.
I fear, though striving hard, I'll fail.
Can I consign a sahib to gaol?

'Sir,' the sergeant's voice breaks in.
'Sahib, vill I now be bringing back
the *chhokra*, so you can begin
to find out who he called as Jack?'
Well, Jack thinks, now it's been said.
It's out, a Jack and a memsahib dead.
It had to come to light, the tale.
No thousand lies would draw a veil
over a scandal such as this.
So, well done, Sergeant *Kya-naam*.   He is woken
It's ... Yes, of course, Bulaki Ram.   from a brown
Well, he's a chap you'd easily miss.   study by Sergeant
But all the same I think that he   What's-his-name.
might be worth keeping close to me.

So, 'Yes,' Jack said, 'bring me the brat.'
I'd better hear just what that shout
consisted of. And after that,
he thinks, a list of all about
the Station with a first name Jack.
There can't be many I'll have to track.
The thought loomed then: however can
I question men whose work began
out here while I was still a baby?
He thrust it down. Don't think of it.
And Guthrie, won't he soon be fit
to do it all himself? Well, maybe.
If I'd time now I'd go and pray
Oh, Lord, take this hard task away.

But there's no time. Yes, now it's duty.
And here's the boy. Thin of chest, legs like sticks,
snotty-nosed, no thing of beauty.
Yet lurking somewhere hard to fix
a bubbling joy when his one gift
comes into play, when he can lift
his head, send in a mindless frothing-out
all that he's heard, a waterspout.
'*Bolo*,' Bulaki Ram's sharp order.
Then, 'No, Jack! No, Jack!'
The cry – her voice – came shrieking back
as from a record, true recorder.
So, yes, it's so. No room for doubt.
Jack felt a long breath sighing out.

The words, Jack thought, had not been quite
the ones Bulaki Ram had said.
But, yes, he got the message right:
someone called Jack and a memsahib dead.
Jack turns to Little Brown Gramophone
to hear, once more, just what he's known
he'd hear again. And it comes back,
Milly's voice, 'No, Jack! No, Jack!'
Reluctantly he starts to think
who in the Station has that name.   Another numbing
And finds, to his bewildered shame,   blow: no one
Jack's a name he cannot link   appears to be
to anyone at all. Not one   called Jack.
called Jack, in truth or fun.

All right, he thought, that's no surprise.
If just plain Jack is one's own name,
then one is bound to recognise
even a stranger's that's the same.
So now I face another task:
I must ask and ask and ask
all the men whose names are John,
or any other Jack-like, Jack-gone
variants on simple Jack. Or
I must find if anyone, for any cause,
has been by Milly-grabbing-claws
styled Jack. A joke. A nickname for
some *Jackass* she once lured to bed?
Some *Jackal*, a biter-love instead?

Then Jack, the tyro, thinks, appalled,
Do women – ladies – really like
to feel sharp teeth ...? But he recalled
a chap he'd met, a man called Pike,
who'd boasted, like that grim-jawed fish,
– and this, he claimed, by their own wish –
he never kissed but his teeth set
in flesh a mark they'd not forget.
So, Marchbanks Mem, had she been such?
Sex-mad? Well, Guthrie told me so,
said if she beckoned just don't go.
But who had gone? Been quick to touch
pitch and – and *want* to be defiled?
Pike, when he'd boasted, too, had smiled.

Was that what Englishmen should do?
Was that what she, dead there, had done?
A lady, memsahib, someone who
should show the way. Oh, decent fun
one could excuse, or even share.
At dances, yes, a shoulder bare
could be caressed. But was there more,
much worse, with her? And it is sure
that if the mystery lasts too long,
and Guthrie cannot leave his bed
then I myself will soon be led
into marshes rank and strong.
What should not be. Mud spattering pride.
And Britons letting down the side.

PART THREE

Snow, a carpet of pure white
with every little footmark showing.
The mystery story at its height
could count on every reader knowing
that any milieu snow-surrounded
meant that the suspects are all rounded
up, or coralled, for Reader-sleuth
to follow clues and reach the truth.
Well, that was fine with bird-marked snow
in wintry North, pure as a nun.
But 'neath, as they say, the tropic sun
how's Reader to be made to know
that only in some laid-down girdle
can dark suspicions spawn and curdle?

Well, how? Perhaps this is the way:
(Reader, suspend some disbelief)
surround our Club with, shall we say,
a high thorn-hedge, a contra-thief.
Within that put our bungalow
beside the Club. *Hé voilà*, snow.
Now, take the time that Milly's shout,
her *No, Jack! No, Jack!* came shrieking out.
The tale was bandied here and there,
and took some hours to reach the police.
Some who were told failed to release
the secret story out of fear.
Or avarice. With such a prize
to hug, that's really no surprise.

But when at length Jack sought to fix
the time of that boy-heard *No, Jack!*
(he knew he'd learnt himself by six)
through painful tracing back and back,
from vague replies, discounting lies,
he found the time of her demise.
At last, he thought, I've got it right.
Counting back, I guess it might
have been – or, no, it must have been
some time near noon. So, satisfied,
he told Bulaki Ram with pride
what now he knew must be the scene
when whoever she'd called Jack
had left that corpse upon her back.

Jack attempts
to fix the
time of
the crime.

Jack thought the sergeant was inclined
to doubt his work. He glared at him.
'Look, *havildar*, that's what I find.
And that's what is.' I'm not so dim,
he almost added. Then held back.
'Sahib, if so, ven that shout *Jack*
the boy is hearing, inside the Club
just seven sahibs.' Aye, the rub,
Jack, Hamlet-quoter, thought at once.
If this chap's right, then one of those ...
'Just seven? Then do you suppose –'
He checked himself. Oh, I'm a dunce.
You would think I'd not been taught
no native should share such a thought.

'Right then, sergeant, on your way.
First things first. What must be done,
quicker the better – hear what I say –
is find if there was anyone,
some servant, with a right to go
inside the Marchbanks bungalow.
Who you find just bring to me.
I'll question him and find if he
saw any sahib about the place.'
'Sir, order has been carried out.
No one is there, not any doubt.
I am not finding even trace.'
Jack frowned. When did I tell the man?
Well, I was dazed when this began.

But let me get it all quite straight,
he thought. The *chhokra* heard that shout
at noon. Where was I then? I hate
to think if I'd been round about
whoever strangled Milly then
– one of only seven men? –
might have seen me and desisted.
Or Milly might have then resisted,
screamed more than that one cry that cost
her her life. But, ah, not so.
I was with Guthrie, had yet to go
to play the match that then he lost.
But at the Club while six souls slept
at noontide's heat, then out one crept.

One crept out with loins enflamed
to go to Milly, rutting goat.
Then she'd taunted? And, ashamed,
had he in fury grabbed her throat?
Or first in rage had wrecked that room?
Then, taunting on, she'd sealed her doom?
And it was then hard strangling hands
had gripped her neck and like bands
of steel stayed there. But not before
she gave that shout *No, Jack! No, Jack!*,
the cry that *chhokra* has brought back,
as if from murder's very door,
for me to hear time and again.
The words implanted in my brain.

But *No, Jack! No, Jack!*
who is that Jack? And is it true
– the ugly thought came cruelly back –   He recalls how
there're really only seven who   his sergeant
were in the Club when Milly died?   has cut down
Which of them then has lied and lied,   the suspects.
or will lie soon of how he slept
when he it was who softly crept
to vent his lust, and then instead
in thwarted rage caused Milly's death?
One cry, and then her choked last breath,
her body broken on that bed?
No, Jack! No, Jack! But who, just who,
is that Jack? What must I do?

But now it's late. Night has long since
wrapped all around in shrouding dark.
Jack's body, every limb, now hints –
no, cries for sleep, to sail the barque
of soothing dreams. But, though so tired,
he cannot rest. He is enmired
in swamp-deep thoughts. He is a-rack,
asking, asking *Who is Jack?*
He had not dared – it was so late –
to question any of those few,
noon-sleepers there and ask just who
had seen whom. That must wait
until next day. Then, mind afresh,
perhaps untangle mesh from mesh.

At 6 a.m, the very dot,
Jack's bearer twitched at his pyjamas,
on the teapoy placed a pot
of tea and two bananas.
Chhota hazari, the little meal.
Jack's hand stole to chin to feel
if bristles still were pricking there.
Not one. All shaved while unaware,
the morning ritual that he'd found
on first arriving, mere tyro,
something hard to undergo.
Yet soon accepted. Tea drunk. A bound
from bed and his bearer, bending low,
dresses him from top to toe.

'Would Sahib go to ride today?'
Britches held up or shorts to choose.
And now Jack thinks with cold dismay
the time is here when I must lose
perhaps what over months I've tried
to gain, respect from in-wool-dyed
old hands. No gallop now in cool
new day, the world around, a jewel.
Instead the task he too well knew
would bring him only hate and scorn.
Elders cheeked by one new-born.
Yet he must discover who
could have done the wicked deed.
Who was that who? And not one lead.

Not one lead. But just one hope.
Guthrie, the victim of the sun,
might he by now be fit to cope,
by saying what he would have done
had he been taking up the case?
Yes, see him now. Then face-to-face
he may with just one pithy word
make all my worries look absurd.
So with no further loss of time,
Jack stands beside the sick man's bed.
At once to find that one hope fled.
Eyes shut, brow hot, a frothy rime
obscuring lips, and body wet
with sullen globules of rank sweat.

'Matron, he looks really ill.
As if – Well ... As –' Jack said.
He thought *If ... If ... What will
I do? If – If Guthrie should be dead.*
Matron, a lady brisk as bee,
barked out a laugh. 'If there should be
another death? Well, is that what
you're thinking? Not a jot
of it. Give us at most two days,
and then you'll see old F.H.R.
up on his feet. Or, that is, bar
the unforeseen. You know God's ways
are often, lad, just quite mysterious.
But sunstroke's never deathly serious.'

Jack left. His heart is in his boots.
No help from Guthrie, and ahead
at least derision, if not hoots
of mocking laughter when instead
of meekly nodding when they spoke,
or modest smiling at each joke,
he takes old India hands to task.
Such questions that I'll have to ask.
He reached the *daftar*, his steps slowing,
and there Bulaki Ram awaits.
'Sahib, are you vishing,' then he states,
'me to come also ven you are going
to funeral?' Jack winced in shame.
I'd forgotten. I'm to blame.

Thank goodness that Bulaki Ram
happened to speak, or otherwise
I would have missed it, and what harm
that would have done. I can't disguise
the state of disarray I'm in.
But, with mind still in a spin,
he mounted bike and hurried home
thinking *Change, then brush and comb.*
Quickly there dons formal kit,
best uniform and Sam Browne belt.
Just in time, thanks heartfelt
(no bearer's help: no time for it).
But at the church he saw the rank
of heads-down mourners. His heart sank.

There, as if some trick of fate
had placed them there in full display,
came passing through the churchyard gate
the seven souls who yesterday
had slept – one not – when there had come
that shout of *No, Jack!* and the dumb
silence. Here, as on parade,
under the church trees' heat-parched shade,
the seven souls. Jack thought: My chance
at least to look at each to see
if I can guess how one can be
by some odd quirk a Jack. Advance
one step at least in my hard quest.
But will light come at my behest?

By coincidence the seven suspects are lined up.

So, first to place upon the slide
under my mental microscope?
(But, though strong-lit, can't they still hide?)
Well, at the grave, grave as a pope,
our Padre, my friend Peter Fox,
simple, jolly, orthodox.
Come, surely not dead Milly's Jack.
Surely he was on his back,
sound, sound asleep when creeping
out from drowsy Club her killer
went, all other suspects sleeping.
A man who's murdered, yet a pillar
of our world he'll seem to be.
But who, but which – yes, which? – is he?

Yet after all it still could be
nice Peter Fox. Who can tell
what lurks, a sullen mystery,
what demon hides within the shell?
Our Padre, who each Sunday preaches
a simple sermon when he teaches
us, if we are willing hearers
(the back pews hold some Christian bearers),
how we ought to live our lives,
how the wicked always perish,
how the good man, sometimes, thrives,
those precepts that we ought to cherish.
A man so plainly on God's side,
did he –? Oh, Lord, with us abide.

No. Turn away. Another slide
under mental microscope.
Though in the end Fox must be tried.
Given, like the others, rope
to hang himself if he's the one.
Here now under Punjab sun
the victim must be huddled quick
to earth. But then in just a tick
I'll have to put each suspect through
such hoops as I can find to test
the lies that each may manifest.
So while I can let me renew
my searching here in stance or face
for just one hint of foul disgrace.

Try Arthur Brent, the engineer,
maker of bridges and of roads.
A man who does. And drinks his beer,
smokes his pipe. On leave, he loads
his gun to shoot a little game.
His hope, at best, a modest fame:
a giant break on the billiard table.
A man, Jack thought, as one I'd label
salt of the earth and decent fellow.
So how could he ...? But underneath
who knows what his genes bequeath?
(*Gene* is a word he wouldn't bellow
out aloud in case it's *ge-ne*,
two syllables to rhyme with *teeny*.)

'Man that is born of woman hath
but a short time to live ...' The sound
remote. *Tell it not in Gath.*
Words and quotation, each rebound
within Jack's head and die away.
Black night faces me today.
Take Arthur. Will, before it's dark,
I have to caution him, embark
on all the business of his trial?
Take him to gaol? Good God, not there,
not to the gaol where natives wear
coarse convict garb, a place so vile
I feel half-sick each time I go
on duty there. Not that. No. No.

But, if it isn't Arthur, who
will I have to put in gaol?
Yes, what it is I have to do
is find the culprit without fail.
As soon as on the coffin there
has rattled dust-dry earth I swear
I'll tackle one of those who stand
here at the graveside, take in hand
my task, however blackly grim.
He looks across to pick out one.
Is that the man? Or him? Or him?
Or, worse, much worse, before I'm done,
the one of all who's not a sahib.
Miss Browne. A woman. Sharp that barb.

Yes, somehow in my mind I've lumped
within the thorn-hedge ring those few
as sahibs, as men. Somehow I jumped
to that when all along I knew
one who was there, and bound to be,
was our Miss Browne. Oh yes, it's she
who's there all day, is working there
from dawn to dusk since in her care
are all the thousand daily chores
that make Club life run smooth and sweet.
Jacqueline Browne, what we eat,
what we drink, clean towels, washed floors,
her charge for years they've been.
Ever efficient Jacqueline.

Jacqueline. But can't that name
be shortened into simple Jack?
So, though a woman, she's to blame?
Can it be it's her whose track
has, so to speak, gone off all wrong?
Jack Steele, the boy, had not been long   He begins to
at school when he was told the Nurse   glimpse what
and Housekeeper did things much worse   may lie behind
than what at night the nastiest boys   the façade.
did with each other in the dorm.
And, though he thinks that's damn bad form,
from time to time the thought annoys
him, rising up, with sounds, with sights,
hot in the stillness of hot nights.

'In the midst of life,' the Padre booms,
'we are in death.' A stab of fear.
Surely in the task that looms
some other answer will appear,
Jack prays, though that is not the prayer
he should be quietly uttering here.
But, poor chap, his shoulders sink
beneath the thoughts that he must think.
Not for him the cosy feelings
the young have viewing someone dead,
*It's sad for them, but I instead
am alive, and life's appealing.*
No. Jack, though young, is firmly caught.
A trap worse than the worst he's thought.

So now, with resolution, he
grabs at one other by the grave.
Who? Which? Any here would be
better than her. Fool or knave,
better than finding in the end
a woman, lady, memsahib bend
her mind to, first, that love
– no, not *love*, dear God above –
and then, when something goes awry ...
So, *fool*, if that's not too unkind
a word to stick on old Plum Duff.
But truth to tell, and it's plain why,
Plum Duff is seen by everyone
as foolish. Nice, of course, but fun.

George Duff, in life an also-ran,
now Secretary of the Club.
Here, as he puts it, 'boy and man'.
Well, at least half-true. The nub
of it is he's gained his post
simply because for much the most
of his life India has been
his home. He came here at 14,
and now he's 60, or all but.
And often he tells anyone
he buttonholes that 'when the sun
goes down for me or I go phut'
(as mostly he describes his end)
'then here I'll rest, God send.'

Jack thinks, if anyone's the killer,
I suppose old Plum's the one
I'd choose. Because he's not that pillar
of the community. Just fun.
In fact, a clown. A walking joke.
We'd spare him more than any bloke
of weight or substance in the life
that we lead here. Nor's there a wife
to complicate a clean arrest.
Not like – it would be darkest night –
District Commissioner Derek Wright.
Arresting him would be a test
even Guthrie well might lack
the guts for. If he's my Jack ...

If that should be, there's Mrs Wright.
If that's the fate that overhangs
her, how would she live another night
when he's in gaol, or if he hangs.
Yes, there. That is the very worst.
By all who knew him I'd be cursed.
Whatever could I find to say
to Wright Memsahib that grimmest day?
Madam, your husband has killed Milly?
I utter that to Mrs Wright,
she'd answer *Steele, you must be tight.*
Or, worse, *Now, boy, you know that's silly.*
No, no nightmare looks more black
if it should prove that Wright is Jack.

And yet ... Well, I should try to think it.
A man's a man, and he might fall,
long for the wicked cup, then drink it.
And somehow I can't see at all
the D.C. and his lady wife
making love now that her life
has passed, has surely passed, its prime.
And, if they don't, there'd come a time
when he, a man with all a man's
strong urges, might find such a one
as Millicent, who's no one's nun,
so tempting that at last she fans
his ardour to a fever pitch.
And in the end he kills the bitch?

But afterwards? Let's think of it. <small>He attempts</small>
He – Jack let's call him and no more – <small>to put himself</small>
creeps back to bed when he has quit <small>into the mind</small>
that murder room, contrives to snore, <small>of the killer.</small>
so no one waking in noon's heat
will know that he has gone to meet
the woman who now lies in death,
the tart he's choked to her last breath.
What deep remorse must he now feel.
And worse: if someone chanced to hear
that *No, Jack!* scream? What fear
will pin him to his bed. That squeal
ringing, ringing, loud and high?
Now he must live a living lie.

Yes, one amongst those seven souls,
Jack thinks, must now be blackly facing
a long life while hot-burning coals
of sharp regrets are searing, tracing
deep paths across his very brain.
I now am also murderer Cain.
But which of them, still by the grave,
is self-condemned for life to slave
as one held by their fears in chains?
Today for them is Number One
of day on day, all the long run
of life ahead, unending pains.
But who – Jack's mind keeps going back –
who is the one that she called Jack?

Is it – Why, it well could be –
Dr Prosser? He's a man.
And, for all he's fat and puffy,
must share all males' since time began
propensity to hot-fired lust.
Though he has always fussed and fussed
like some old dame, but still perhaps
inside the tabby heart that taps
as gently as a ticking clock
there lurks a tiger, ever drooling.
A lust that he has thought of cooling
– be coarse – by giving Milly cock.
But, stop. It cannot be the quack:
no one ever calls him Jack.

Yet still in theory one who might
have gone, at noontime heat, by stealth
to creep away in midday night
and sup, in hope, of Milly's wealth
of female wiles and lover-games.
Six thought about of seven names.
Now Edward Carter, last in line.
A planter, 28 or 9.
Something always hard to grasp
about the chap. A bit aloof.
Inside his shoe a cloven hoof?
No sign of it, no sign to rasp
the senses. Yet, well, isn't there
something too flashy in his air?

And now earth with a gentle patter
falls on the coffin. Dust to dust.
The mourners now begin to scatter,
forgetting soon poor Milly's lust.
Except for one? One at the grave
who yesterday took her and gave
her limp dead body one shake more.
Someone she'd touched upon the raw.
Someone, yes, it has to be,
who went to her, heart fiercely pounding,
and saw her, shortly, turn and rounding
on them, spit out words that she
knew well would sting like any whip.
Then hands enraged, the deadly grip.

PART FOUR

Jack sees them go. The Padre first,
then Derek Wright beside his wife
(she not on my list), lips pursed
in disapproval of the life
that Milly led. Next, pompous fusspot
Dr Prosser. And then we've got
Jacqueline. A woman killing?
No. Yet was Milly willing
to do that thing with anyone
of either sex? Then next to go,
Edward Carter. It could be so.
Then Plum Duff, the man of fun.
And, last of seven I've been sent,
that decent fellow, Arthur Brent.

In his mind
he once again
lines up
the suspects.

Jack knows his moment now is here.
One of the seven he must see.
This is the time. Now: not near.
Yet how he longs for it to be
miraculously not his task.
'Ah, Steele, something I must ask.'
The D.C. There. Commanding, tall,
in himself comprising all
that British rule depends upon.
Stern, unbending, blankly just.
One who holds a world in trust.
He's seen his wife go walking on.
At attention Jack, undone,
admits his task has now begun.

He quakes, a little, in his shoes
facing this man he's scarcely seen.
Or only when he states his views
in court where Jack on duty's been
a witness, judgments cutting through
the verbiage, the lies men spew
to wriggle out of their wrongdoing.
A god. An angel, fire-pursuing
all the wicked. None escape
the law that Britain's brought the land.
More just than kind, Jack thought, and
later half-took back the words. Red tape,
he glimpsed, and regulations
keep men on course as well as nations.

'Well, Steele, this is an evil day
for all of us, and more for you
with Guthrie there in the sick bay.
So, tell me, is there any clue
to who committed that foul act?
A native, let's not baulk the fact,
must be to blame. But, tell me, you –'
Jack interrupted, dared to do.
But truth must out. 'No, sir, not so.
The fact is, there can be no doubt,
the killer, at noon, came creeping out
from the Club. Sir, it's a blow,
but, for certain reasons, I
am sure of that.' 'Come, Steele, why?'

At once Jack's in a quandary.
Must he reveal that cry *No, Jack!*
when Mr Wright's one who might be
that very Jack? Or, to go back
on his self-made vow to hide
that fact until he can decide
which it is of the seven who
slept in the Club is called Jack too.
But the question has been put.
The D.C.'s asked it *Come, Steele, why?*
and he's a man you cannot try
to slide past, treading pussyfoot.
Epitome of what's correct.
True and tough and, yes, direct.

'Sir, it's like this, and, if you please,
don't tell a soul what's come to light.
As Mrs Marchbanks on her knees
felt the strangler's hands grow tight
she uttered one despairing cry.
No, Jack! she screamed. And that is why
I know no native is to blame.
It has to be one Jack by name.
Then, sir, there is one other fact.
When she cried out it was a time
when, and this is certain, I'm
afraid, with the thorny hedge intact,
just seven sahibs were sleeping there
in the Club. And, sir, I fear ...'

'Fear what? Speak up, speak up, my boy.'
'Sir, of those seven one was you.'
'Yes, you're right. On my *charpoy*
dare say I snored. Right, I knew
when I first saw you that we'd found
a chap who underneath was sound.'
Jack felt a glow of pure delight.
Not always when you do what's right
do you find you've come out top.
So now in the D.C.'s books
– no need to walk on tenterhooks –
am I the pick of the new crop?
But then the rocket falls unlit.
He knows he has not done with it.

All right, he's bearded Mr Wright,
said he's a suspect. But there's more.
Still the bullet's there to bite.
He's got to ask – put in his oar –
if Derek is his only name,
or if – once more there is the same
dilemma there – he's, too, a John
(that's Jack). But, no, his daring's gone.
It sparked. But all too brief its airing.   Too young, he
He flunks the test. Well, he postpones it.   fails to press
Jack, he'll ask which others own it.   hard enough.
And so he's silent, simply swearing
that if at last he finds no Jack,
he'll stiffen sinews and come back.

'Now, Steele, there's something else to say.
I think you may not actually know
that here to us within a day
or so – whether we like or no –
an M.P.'s coming on a trip.
Catch us squarely on the hip
with this murder still unsolved
and he may think that we're involved
in every sort of filth and muck.
That, in short, the place is rotten.
But if, by then, it's all forgotten,
or, at least with any luck,
dealt with, disposed of, neat and tidy ...
The fellow will be here by Friday.

Friday? But that's just days away,
Jack thinks. How will I ever, ever
manage? Guthrie out of play,
and up till now I have never
had a really decent case.
There was one, quite commonplace.   He recalls
I'd caught ten men – I felt a thrill –   his sergeant
with the victim bleeding still,   solving for him
and questioned each. *I do not know.*   a simple case.
Ten times the sullen answer came.
At last, to my appalling shame,
I said that I would have to go.
Bulaki Ram stayed on behind.
There'll be no marks. Your man I'll find.

'And one thing more,' Wright Sahib said.
'Don't think I mean to interfere,
but police routine? On that head
are you all right? Guthrie not there,
can you manage on your own?'
'I think so, sir.' Jack had grown
pretty proud of that word *sound*
bestowed on him, and so had found
self-confidence. 'My *havildar*,
a first-class chap, Bulaki Ram,
knows the ropes. Not much harm
will come to me, I think.' 'Ah,
word of warning there, young Steele.
From him ... all this ... best to conceal.'

'Of course, sir. F.H.R. was saying
once that we're on show all day
and all night too. They're there weighing
us up and we must also weigh
our actions in that constant light.'
'Yes, Steele, F.H.R. is right,
though you're a little off-beam here.
No native weighs us. They don't dare.
But, true, they gossip, love to find
a white man not behaving well.
That's why I thought it best to tell
you to keep all this behind
closed doors. Not a word to Ram
that could cause the slightest harm.'

Jack saluted, went away,
ready now to do his best.
Only soon to wish that they,
the six now subject of his quest,
were somehow less intimidating.
I'll try, he thought. But he was hating
doing what he had to do,
poking, prying, pointing to ...
Bulaki Ram at strict attention,   At his office,
'Sahib, inside he is there vaiting.'   unexpectedly
Waiting? Who? Jack's just berating   he finds
the fellow for some damn invention   he has begun.
when smartly he brings out a name.
'Brent sahib. I ask. He came.'

Arthur Brent. But how did he,
Bulaki Ram, know I must meet
each one in turn? Well, let that be.
Now I must, in Guthrie's seat,
ask Arthur what I know I should.
Will I find truth or sly falsehood?
'Arthur, good morning. I just thought
I'd have a word. My chap brought
you here because at any cost
we don't want things to get about.'
'Things? What things?' 'Now, please don't shout.'
But shouting ...? And his temper lost?
A guilty conscience? Straight away
have I struck gold? A stag at bay?

'Shouting? I'm not shouting. Look,
what the hell's all this about?'
'Arthur, I know my fellow took
a liberty in bringing you. No doubt
he thought that I had said
I had to see you. Well, dead
Milly Marchbanks' corpse demands
if not vengeance, well, commands
the truth be found. So I've to ask
each person who might have been there
at round about that midday where
they were in fact.' 'What, unmask
the murderer? You? You pup.
Listen, boy, just stop such gup.'

But Jack's undaunted. Threats, he thinks.
Have I, in one, laid hands upon
the killer? That hot wrath just stinks.
Is it pure luck that Ram has gone
to Arthur Brent first of the six?
But can I now defeat his tricks?
Because it's plain he's no intention
to spend his life in black detention.
No, if Arthur really is my man
he's going to fight me all the way.
So how, how, can I make him say
he did the thing? Well, if I can
I must somehow trip his heels.
Say something ... What? So he misdeals.

An idea comes into his mind.
A ruse that might ... Give it a try.
The nub of it is how to find
who Milly meant just when that cry
No, Jack! No, Jack!
broke from her lips. So try this tack ...
Will this tell me who Milly meant?
Sharply across the desk he leant
and said, 'Now, please, give me a break,
Jack –' *Jack*. There he'd named him so.
Would he in heat just let it go?
Not see, unthinking, his mistake?
If so, then Milly called him Jack.
In all his protests one wide crack.

'Jack? Jack? Who do you think
you're talking to? That's not my name.
Look, I don't want to make a stink,
but I wonder what's your game.
You question me as if I am
a murderer, plainly when some damn
native killed poor Millicent.
I tell you I am innocent
as any new-born babe. Now, why
has it got into your head
a white man left poor Milly dead?
It's plain that she was strangled by
a native, that some bloody black –'
Can I tell him? That cry *Jack*?

'No, Arthur. And I'm sorry if
it seemed as if it could be you.
But I'm afraid there's not a whiff
of evidence, no, not a clue
to say a native is to blame.
I can't say more. I must claim
a policeman's right to hold his tongue.
Believe me, if I could have hung
this on any but a sahib, I'd
have grabbed the chance. I know full well
the scandals natives love to tell
in the bazaar. So we must hide
what's happened quietly as we may.
Yet truth must come to light of day.'

'Steele, I'll take your word for it.
I'm sorry I got in a bate.
But I feel I've done my bit
year in, year out, early, late,
for India. And to find a crime
that must – it seemed so at the time –
be natives' work put down to me,
well, it got my goat, you see.'
'Of course, old man, quite understood.
I was to blame. Not telling you
at once just how a certain clue
tells me no native ever could
have done this thing that's surely thrown
as dark a shadow as we've known.'

Brent left, Jack's hand much shaken.
And Jack sat thinking who to see.
Now off his list one more's been taken,
which of five is it to be?
A knock. His door is pushed aside.
Bulaki Ram there holds it wide,
and in steps, smiling, Edward Carter.
The emblem of his Alma Mater,
the old school tie he always wears.
'You wanted me, old boy, that so?'
Jack tells Bulaki Ram to go.
'Well, yes. Yes, in a way.' (Jack cares
less for truth than easiness.)
Bulaki's got me in a mess.

Heck, I'm ready not at all
to question yet another suspect.
Once again, well, won't I fall
flat on my face? Lose what respect
I've got? Which, truth to tell,
is not a lot. Why the hell
did damn Bulaki wheel him in?
Still, as he's here I must begin.
'Look, Edward, won't you take a pew.
It's Millicent, of course, that I
must ask – well ... ask you why –'
A sudden thought. Without a clue,
why don't I ...? 'Listen, Ed,
I know you've taken her to bed.'

The daring move. Will it pay off?
Edward's the one who, really might
be most likely ... Young ... A cough.
'I'm sorry, Jack, did I hear right?'
Jack blushes, but still has to plough
on. He's said the words and now
there is no way to take them back.
(Again he hears that cry *No, Jack!*)
'I said I knew there was this thing
you had with Milly. You know what
I mean. Affair. I know it's not
my business if you had a fling.
But now, well, you see, it is.'
Edward fingers that tie of his.

'But surely it was just some black –'
'No. It's not. I can't say why.
But take my word.' And once more Jack
asks *Did Carter see her die?*
Edward sits there, and his hand
plays with his tie. 'Please understand,
what it is I'm going to tell
must be our secret. And, oh hell,
you haven't any right to know.
But I suppose I must confess
it all, however much distress
it causes me. Like Wilde and Co.,
my sexual urge is not at all
female directed. I'm what they call

a homo, pansy, nancy boy.
I'm one of those. Well, go on, laugh,
sneer, sit there smiling and enjoy
my discomfort, torn in half
between confessing to my sin
or letting you think that you can pin
Milly's death on Edward Carter.'
Jack's thunderstruck. A martyr
sits before him. And he never
for one moment guessed there,
underneath, there lay, laid bare,
– Edward, who ... who would ever ...? –
lay a troubled double life.
Wilde, after all, too had a wife.

Would Edward one day, back from leave,
bring with him proudly a new bride?
A girl he'd hope would then deceive
his cronies, friends, the while he tried
perhaps to end this fearful vice
that gripped him now? To use some nice
girl whom he hoped would somehow cure him?
Or to use – could she endure him? –
her as a shield or a disguise?   He finds yet
Here was a thought that did appal: another surface
that underneath the surface all   no more than
might be a mass of squalid lies.   a surface.
All right, if it was just this chap ...
But black all under red-marked map?

And now there came another knock,
one different from Bulaki's tap.
Reeling still from Carter's shock,
Jack sensed some trouble in the rap.
Before he'd even called out *Come*
the D.C. entered. Jack was dumb.
He sat there in his boss's seat,
failed to rise, failed to greet
the great man as he ought to do.
Carter stood. 'Look, Jack, I'll go.
And, if you can ... Well, you know.'
He left. The D.C. asked, 'Who
was that?' 'One, Carter, sir.' At last
Jack broke the trance that held him fast.

'With reference to our little chat,'
the D.C. said. 'There's one thing more
I thought perhaps – well, perhaps that
should be said.' Glance to the door.
'Just making sure no one can hear.
What I've got to make quite clear,
you see, is what the state of things
– when mud's thrown, well, it clings –
in the Marchbanks ménage was.
You've heard the gossip, all too true,
alas. But not a thing for you
to meddle in. Well, just because
these things occur there is no need
to pay them any undue heed.

But, you know, well, old Mike knew.   <small>Another</small>
And we knew too just how she went on.   <small>revelation</small>
And we knew that, that is, that he knew   <small>adds to his</small>
how Millicent was rather bent on   <small>troubles.</small>
taking fellows to her bed.
Well, it's tricky, as I've said.
And, of course, it's just not done,
to go to bed with anyone.
White, of course. But she did it.
Well, better not spread it abroad
any more – I mean, good Lord,
although we knew, of course we hid it.
I hope you understand, old man.
Just keep it quiet, far as you can.'

'Yes, sir,' said Jack. Wright gone, he sat
just where he was and puzzled hard.
He felt that here was something that
somehow put him on his guard,
some link between what he'd just heard
and Ed's confession, which had stirred
him to his very depths. The two
both somehow seemed to say that, do
all you could to keep the right,
what was above, the ought-to-be,
was only there for men to see.
While underneath, below the light,
the ought-not waited, whip and spur.
Was that the way things really were?

PART FIVE

At length Jack thrust aside the threat
that he'd felt lurking there in wait,   He does his best
the thought that all that he had met   to reject the
in India here did not relate   dark thoughts.
to what was so. It was a face,
and underneath ...? No, his place
simply to act. And this he knows.
He knows that he is one of those
whose life, whose training, all has gone
into his niche in that one race
destined to rule, awarded grace
– if you like – to sit there on
the seats of power. To guide the poor,
the lesser breeds without the law.

So, action now. No sitting slack.
An obstacle is looming there.
But it is there – that cry *No, Jack!* –
to be got over. Do and dare.
I captained once the First XI
so finding which of six, no, seven
(six sahibs and, don't forget, one she)
was in lust called Jack must be
a task that falls to me the leader
that once I was. Myself before
my India life. So, once more
I must be such, and not a pleader
for sympathy because of what
I have just learnt. No. Not. Not.

Thrust aside these darts of doubt
sprung up in me like moaning ghosts.
Ghosts from the future. Cast them out.
No, justify all Britain's boasts.
Forget, deny that Underneath.
Those evil lies which we bequeath
one to another down the years,
shut them away. To hell with fears
that all our surface sureties
are crazy-built on filthy slime,
that we're pretending all the time,
a card-house held to be what is.
No. We are here to act.
What seems to be must be the fact.

Jack, that resolution made,
knows what it is he's got to do.
Seek commonsense, a spade a spade.
And there is no one better to
give him a dose of certainty
than F.H.R. Just pray that he
this morning's in a fitter state.
His sun-wrecked ship with all its freight
of manliness and long-held lore
sailing once more, if only through
coast waters, and that all its crew
of maxims, mottoes, yes, and pi-jaw
are at their posts, each ready to
lay down the law, say what to do.

Full of hope, an end to whining,
Jack sets out to see his boss.
And finds the sun no longer shining.
Grey cloud stretching right across
the once bright sky, to his alarm.
But then he meets Bulaki Ram.
'Sahib, monsoon is on its vay.'
'The first for me. But, gosh, the day
is sultry hot.' And I'm sweating
like a pig, worse than before
when I thought the sun was more
than I could stand, though not regretting
that I was working in its blaze,
would be beneath it all my days.

In Guthrie's ward Jack's hopes soon sink.
The red-faced man gone blotchy grey.
Jack scarcely knows what he should think.
Guthrie lost, and day on day.
No help then when his help's most needed.
He looks down. The face all beaded
with great drops of oily sweat.
Oh, Guthrie, will you never get –
And then he sees one open eye,
bright blue, alive, and, if not clear,
clear enough for every fear
to melt away. 'Well, Steele, why
are you so late in coming round?'
Jack's heart gives just one joyous bound.

'I'm sorry, sir. But do you know
what's happened while you've been so ill?'
'How could I, lad, I've been in no
fit state for anything. Now, will
you bring me up to date *ek dum*?
Just tell me, lad, and then I'll come.'
'You will, sir. That's the best of news.
I've had to stand, sir, in your shoes
when something very bad's occurred.'
'What is it, lad?' He tries to rise.
But then, although now both his eyes
are open wide, they're swiftly blurred.
He sinks back down, his fire all gone.
His eyes stay shut, his face is wan.

Jack waits. Can Guthrie once again
look up at him, light in those eyes?
Or will he sink, subside in pain?
Jack wishes it were otherwise,   He sees now
that he could cope without advice,   that the task
no lamb set up for sacrifice.   will be his alone.
But then at last the patient stirs.
Dead hopes Jack swiftly disinters.
At least, he thinks, I may learn how,
with those seven not-Jack souls
with alibis, to see those holes
detectives always spot somehow.
Guthrie will know. At least he'll guide
me from his bed. Then woe betide ...

And now at last, with blue eyes wide,
it's, 'Tell me, lad, but make it slow.
Give me a moment to decide
if I am up to it. Right, go
ahead. It's murder? Bad, you say?
So who's been murdered? In what way?'
'Sir, it was the Marchbanks widow.'
'Milly? Murdered? Who did – Oh!
My head, my head! A minute, Steele,
let me draw breath.' Jack waits again.
He sees that face cut deep by pain.
Am I right now if I reveal
not the details, though they're gory,
but the heart of my black story?

'Now, lad, give a full report,
Rudyard's *honest serving-men.*
Take each in turn and when you've thought
spit out the who, the where, the when.'
Jack took a moment then to think
and when he had – pause at the brink –
told Guthrie every single thing,
forcing himself at last to bring
out the fact that weighed and weighed
him down, that cry *No, Jack!*
and what it proved. From his back
at last he felt the dark cloud fade.
Now Guthrie, even if bed-panned,
was there to hold him by the hand.

The blue, blue eyes, now needle-sharp,
looked up at Jack. 'Next in to bat?
You've bowled out Brent, and I'll not carp
about the way you handled that.
And Carter – Well, yes, that I knew.'
Then for an instant Jack's doubts drew
up once again. Was I alone
the innocent when all had known?
That ought-not-to-be is that
which everyone but Jack Steele knows?
But stop it. No, such thoughts as those
I must suppress, yes, stop them flat.
I'm getting orders to obey.
Guthrie, what's he going to say?

'Right, lad, there's just one thing for it.
You know what there is still to do.
A gentleman? Forget, ignore it.
Lie. Show anger. If need be, coo
like a bloody turtle-dove.
Or, with the woman, well, make love,
if that alone will break her down.
Be a bully. Play the clown.
Somehow you have got to learn
if any one of those inside
that circling thorn-hedge lied and lied.
Just go to them, each one in turn
and talk. Yes, talking is the thing
to catch the conscience of the King.'

The King? What's this? Good heavens, where –
What the hell is it he's saying?
But, yes, he's quoting. It's Shakespeare.
It's *Hamlet*, yes. What is he playing
at? Never heard him quote a word.
Jesus, this is too absurd.
He's suddenly begun to rave.
And I was hoping that he'd save
me. *Hamlet,* who'd have thought
he even knew a line of it?
Wait. I think that he's a bit
calmer now. Perhaps he's brought
his wandering thoughts back home again.
If he speaks now, mad or sane?

'I'm sorry, lad, I think that I
must have been somewhere far away.
Now, what was there – What was in my
head? Something that I had to say ...
Ah, yes. I think I've got it now.
It's when you've found him, how
you'll have to manage things.
I won't be there to dance the strings.
Or not if you're as quick as you
ought to be. What day is this?
Caught in a fever a chap can miss
a week or more. You know who
comes here on Friday?' 'An M.P.,
so I was told by the D.C.'

'And when is Friday? You know, I think
it's coming soon.' 'Sir, it's tomorrow.'
'Oh, God, my head. Some of that drink.'
Jack hands him it, and sees with sorrow
that the eyes once more are glazed.
Is he sane now? Or still crazed?
He takes the glass, puts back its beaded
muslin cover. What was needed
he has done. He dares to hope
the cooling drink has done its work,
brought back the man who seems to lurk
just underneath, who tries to grope
to daylight through the fever's fire.
The Guthrie whom he can admire.

'Now listen, Steele, and listen well.
When you've learnt just who it was
you'll have to say – My head. Oh, hell.'
His gritted teeth. 'Look, just because
you may be wrong, you must make sure.
But, once you have, no waiting for
the dregs of proof. No one must ever
come to court. Remember, never.
So what it is you've got to do
is see that it's the decent thing
they do, for England and the King.
Whichever one is found by you,
you're the man who has to see
they shoot themselves. You follow me?'

Shoot themselves? And I'm to see
that they do that? For God's sake, how?
And does he really ...? Or is he
once more half-mad? Or is it now
that he is sane? And this is what
the Raj demands? That one must not
let down the side, not even if
one dies for it? Always the stiff
upper lip? With a gun
placed to your apprehensive ear?
Or in the mouth? Should it be there?
Is that the way? Is that what's done?
Am I – with whom? – to seal that pact?
Am I– Am I to watch the act?

A new, harder
duty bewilders
him yet more.

Imagine me with, say, Plum Duff,
if it should turn out he's the one.
Will I have courage, gall, enough
to tell him he must use the gun?
Or if it's Edward Carter, though
he wears that tie of his and so
should be prepared just to obey?
The Padre – him? – what could I say
if under his dog-collar there's
a lustful man who in the end ...?
Or Mr Wright? God above send
he's not the one. But, say, he bares
his soul to me, then how could I
tell him his duty is to die?

Or Jacqueline, if it is her,
could I insist a woman kill
herself? Well then, would I prefer
it proves that Arthur fits the bill,
that decent fellow, nice as pie?
Or Dr Prosser, one whom I
– now no time to tell a lie –
dislike as pompous and too plump?
Say, if I talk to him and pump
him hard for all I'm worth and find
he went to Milly and that his
pride was stung? Out of his mind
he strangled her? Would I yet be
able to tell him that – That he ...?

His thoughts a-whirl, now Jack looks down
at Guthrie who, it seems, is sleeping.
Was he truly sane just now? A frown.
Whichever, now it's time for keeping
those rendezvous he's told me to.
To talk and talk with each one who
could have gone to Milly then,
and somehow find how it was when
they crept in noon-heat from their bed
inside the Club, and, darting glances
left and right, savouring the chances
that to Milly's bed had led,
crept on. Jack, too, now creeps away.
Is halted when a voice calls 'Hey!

You there! Steele, now if you please
I'd like a word.' The Civil Surgeon,   <small>Encountering</small>
plump and pompous, quite at ease.   <small>Dr Prosser, he</small>
Jack feels his new-come doubts all burgeon. <small>learns one more</small>
Must I gossip, talk and chat   <small>disconcerting fact.</small>
already? Hope this moment that
some word of mine will send a dart
of light to shine right to the heart
of it all? 'Now, look here, Steele,
Guthrie's a man who's very sick,
and I must say it's pretty thick
of you to pester if you feel
you're not up to what you're facing.'
Jack bridles, feels his heart is racing.

'Doctor, you're doing me a wrong.
I had to seek for some advice.
If I had simply gone along,
made an arrest, then in a trice
just as soon as the D.C. heard
he'd say a junior had not stirred
himself to state to F.H.R.
what the facts of the matter are.'
'The facts?' The doctor's face goes white.
'You're telling me that now you know
who killed poor Milly? Is that so?'
Jack pauses, thinks can this be right?
Is Prosser's attitude quite what
an innocent's should be? Or not?

What to ask him? What to say?
How to find if cheeks gone pale
mean much or nothing? Well, come what may
I'll question him, and if I fail
I fail. Here goes. 'Of course, sir, I
can't make you give the reasons why
you may have been –' 'Now listen, boy,
are you attempting to annoy?
How dare you treat me with contempt.
You think that I'm a poor old drunk.
Well, listen, lad, don't you attempt
that line with me. I think you funk
telling someone to their face
that they are simply a disgrace.'

Drunk? Of course, poor Jack now thinks.
Why wasn't it I guessed before?
Good heavens, actually his breath stinks
of brandy and it's little more
than 9 a.m. 'Oh, Doctor, please,'
he quickly says for fear he'll freeze
to silence, dammed all talking
(I'm a hunter, and I'm stalking),
'don't think that to a senior man
I'd speak without respect. It's just
that I've been given certain trust,
and I must honour if I can
all that's been reposed in me.'
Prosser glared. 'Thass as may be.'

But some of his drunk bellicosity
seems as if it's left him now.
So Jack, with rapid reciprocity,
smiles at him, but wonders how
to carry on this much fraught chat
because he has just realised that
a man as spirits-soaked as this
could easily have longed to kiss
very willing Millicent.
To kiss? Jack searches in his mind
for a word – what can I find? –
that tells the truth, no innocent
a fudging. No, for once don't duck.
To hell hypocrisy. It's *fuck*.

Right. What if Prosser, though he's fat,
is my man? Did he ...? Think what
must have happened, and not that
which the surface shows. Yes, not
the outward show, but what there lies
beneath. The truth. So ... His eyes
alight with lust and heating drink,
did he approach? And did he think
she, ready to take on all-comers,
would welcome him with open arms?
Would offer him, though fat, her charms?
Charms? No. Her forty summers
used, but still so very willing,
open legs. Not arms. The killing

followed as the day the night.
A fat drunk spurned, or worse
plain mocked. To her a sight
for laughter. Then his deep-sprung curse,
and fury flooding through and through
his whole fat frame, and drunken too.
And then the reaching, strangling hands.
He acts, but hardly understands
what it is that he has done.
And have I understood it now?
Have I guessed right? Guessed just how?
Now I have at last begun
to see a Doctor, mender, healer,
as a drunken double-dealer?

'You smile. You dare to smile at me.'
Suddenly as he had calmed,
Prosser – brandy with his tea
in bed? – turned red with rage. Alarmed,
Jack blinks and takes a sharp pace back.
It's him? For him she yelled *No, Jack!*?
But then the doctor swung away,
snorted, 'Boy, I'll say good-day,'
and disappeared behind the door
marked *Civil Surgeon*. A bolt clicked.
Jack wondered then: have I been tricked?
Has he fled, escaped before
the treacherous drink led him on to
confess to what was – was it? – true?

Should I thunder on that door?
Insist on questioning the man?
At once came doubts, and even more.
What questions are there that I can
put to him? In truth, just one.
What is it, Doctor, you have done?
Did he creep out while deep in sleep
the others lay? And did he creep
to that sun-drenched bungalow?
Attempt with Milly to make love?
Get repulsed? Oh, God above,
I cannot ask while I don't know
if there's a way he'll be called Jack.
No, to my start I must go back.

PART SIX

Yes, Jack thinks, there are still three
I've hardly talked to, and it's right
to see them first when one may be
a Jack somehow, and still I might
somehow (again!) discover which.
Plum Duff, the Padre or a bitch
who might have brought herself to do
with Milly – No, that can't be true.
So, weighed with thought, Jack makes his way
to Plum Duff's office in the Club.
To talk. Talk, ah, there's the rub.   He presses on,
What on earth to find to say   but there are
so that somehow Plum reveals   challenges he
what every murderer conceals.   still ducks.

'Well, young Steele, how goes it then?'
Plum, affable, easy, bit of a bore.
How to – A lightning flash. Yes. When
just some minutes past I saw
that door shut blankly in my face
on it was more ... Thoughts race.
Yes, under *Civil Surgeon* there
was his name. How very queer
it did not register just then.
But it was there, plain to be seen.
And first a *J*. What's that *J* mean?
J. Norman Prosser. All the men
entitled – to give him the *Norman*.
But that *J*? Can the poor man

hope to hide that he is John?
And Milly, did she call him Jack?
Enough to base a case upon?
Should I this minute hurry back,
accuse him to his face and see
how he takes it? Him and me,
in single combat, man to man?
Trip him up? See if I can?
No, talk to Plum, don't rush away.
And then he's asked me how it goes.
Can't brush him off. Heaven knows
what he would think if I don't stay.
Don't let him feel that I've no time
for someone clearly past his prime.

'How does it go? Not well to date.
I'll be quite frank. I've come to know
that at the time' – Prosser can wait –
'of Milly's death there were, it's so,
only seven in the Club. And, of course,
the compound hedge no one could force.
This is round noon. No getting past
it, one of those, seemingly fast
asleep ... Well, one of those must be –'
Plum's head jerks up. 'Oh gosh, my boy,
you're in a stew. But don't be coy.
You're thinking one of those is me.'
'Good heavens, no,' Jack finds he's said.
'Well, thanks. But still poor Milly's dead.'

'Well, yes, she is, and, worse for me,
F.H.R. is sick and so
all those seven I must see
whether I believe or no
that they could do that awful thing.
And none of them – well, here's the sting –
is, when you look, the sort of chap
who'd rat-like enter in that trap,
who'd slink to Milly, well, for sex.'
'Ah. Now, old son, don't be too sure.   One more
My view, there's no accounting for   surprise for
what happens when the pecker pecks.   the innocent.
But, listen, Jack, don't hesitate
to ask me what's my sexual state.'

'Oh, gosh. Well, I – Well, yes. Oh, gosh.'
'Come now, Jack, you've surely learnt
that, though they talk a lot of tosh,
most chaps are willing to get burnt
like moths at any candle-flame.
Old or young, it's all the same.'
'Well, yes. Yes, I suppose you're right.'
'All right then, I'll admit at night
even through this aged frame
there runs hot blood, and dirty thoughts.
Yes, even what at Home the courts
would send me down for.' In God's name,
Jack thinks, in God's name, stop.
You're old enough to be my Pop.

'But tell me of your early days,'
he quick butts in. 'You didn't marry,
am I right?' 'Does that amaze
you, you young dog? Do you carry
a photo of some girl at Home
next to your heart, swear not to roam
whatever chances may arise?
Well, it may come as some surprise
to you to learn that not all men
feel that with marriage their whole life
would be wrapped up and that a wife
is be-all, end-all too, that when
leaving the altar constant bliss
follows the first sweet wedded kiss.'

Plum Duff gives Jack a modest grin.
'No, Nature's made some few of us
perpetual bachelors. It's no sin
to dislike women for their fuss
and fret and need to be caressed.
Oh, no, my boy, I see you've guessed
that I'm a homo. Well, I'm not.
As to sex, I'll tell you what
excites me, if you want to know.
You've heard of Hamir, Aleem-din?
I see you don't know what I mean.'
Jack feels a hot blush grow and grow.
I've been stupid, dull and dumb.
I've underestimated Plum.

'You've got me there, I must admit.
I know those two names ought to mean
something to me. Not a bit.
Who did you say? Er – Aleem-din?'
'Urdu poet, Jack, my boy.
No need for you to sound so coy.
Half the chaps around don't know
their Hamid from their own big toe.
But take a tip from me and learn
Urdu. Then that poetry,
which means, well, all-in-all to me,
may come to be a light to burn
when all is dark and drear around.
That's when I wallow in its sound.'

Jack tells Plum Duff he'll have a try,
and thinks how odd what I discover.
But then, just as he says good-bye
to this unlikely poetry lover,
he realises there's something more
he's got to ask, what's at the core
of his inquiry: *Are you Jack?*
And somehow I've not learnt the knack   Inwardly
of idle talk on a private matter.   he curses
There are some chaps – I've met a few –   his lack of
who can ask of someone who   savoir–faire.
they scarcely know, as so much chatter,
matters of such secrecy
that if I asked them, well, I'd pee.

Or so at least that's what he thinks.
But now, once more, that *No, Jack!* cry
rings in his head, twirls and twinks.
He hears once more the little spy
outside the Marchbanks bungalow
repeat the words, the *No, Jack, no!*
It is the single clue he's got.
He must pursue it, or he's not
the man he hopes he'll prove to be.
So now, now at this very minute
he must ask Plum. Right, now begin it
somehow, or I'll find that he
has wandered off, my chance has gone.
'I say, Plum, is ... Well, is John ...

Is John your name?' Oh, how crude.
How could I blurt it out like that?
Old Plum will think I'm just damn rude.
But, no, Plum Duff's reply comes pat.
'John? John? What makes you think
that I'm a John?' Jack starts to shrink,
embarrassed as a fellow who's
belched aloud as food he chews.
But Plum Duff is quite unfazed.
'No, my name's George, simple and plain.
George was I christened, can't complain.
But, lad, you seem to be amazed.'
'Amazed? Oh, no. But is George all?'
'Yes, George alone, no Peter, Paul,

nor Mike, nor Tony and not Jack,
or any other name, save Plum.'
Jack now is taken quite aback.
He stands there, almost gawping, dumb.
Is what Plum's said a cunning ploy?
Has he been told, or guessed, the boy
heard Milly's cry, that dreadful *No*?
And did he put that *Jack* in so
I'd believe it can't be him?
Oh God, this is so complicated.
Does it mean that I am fated
at every turn to feel so dim?
But, no. No, I must put my trust
in intuition's way. I must.

And so Jack leaves the Urdu buff,
says to himself I'll scratch him out.
After all, I've troubles enough
without reviving each last doubt.
Heavens, how my poor head aches,
as if the sun that bakes and bakes
this awful land – No. *Awful's* wrong.
India I love, however strong
its sun, or, what is coming soon
– those looming clouds make that quite clear –
the pouring rain that spear on spear
will wet us through, the swift monsoon.
But onwards now. Who's next to ask?
A sudden dread. Oh God, my task.

Just two more I have yet to see
and question. And, yes, one's a priest,
the Padre. And the other? She –
she's a woman. So which is least
likely to plunge me deep in mire?
Peter Fox, whom I admire
for keeping God within the church?
Or Jacqueline? An inner lurch
now tells him she would be the worst.
Right then, it's her I'll tackle now.
At once sweat springs on to his brow.
But – my rule – the worst take first.
Eyes front, face set, he seeks her out.
But what am I to talk about?

Guthrie has told him talk's the way
to bit by bit worm out some fact
that, seen aright, will – or, well, may –
bring to light that fatal act.
But Jacqueline he's scarcely met
or talked to. *Well, I may look wet,*   **He admits to**
but really women shut me up   **himself now his**
as if I was the merest pup.   **inexperience.**
Well, so I am, Jack now admits.
In school I only talked with chaps
a year ago. So, well, perhaps
it's not, you know, so strange if it's
hard for me to talk to girls.
And Jacqueline? All priss and pearls.

The very pink of femaleness
is how Jack sees the suave Miss Browne.
So aren't I bound, he thinks, to mess
up any interview? One frown
at something not at all well said
and I'll stand there and wish me dead.
And if my aim's to dig down deep,
I've got to ask and ask and keep
on asking till I really know
just what she is and what she feels.
Find questions such that each reveals
yet deeper depths. But if I go
along that path – 'Oh, what's it now,
Bulaki Ram?' He wipes his brow.

Try not to let a native see
I'm weak, or guess my forehead sweat
comes not from just the heat, as he
will think, but from unsettled debt.
Embarrassment so deep and thick
I cannot check. No mental trick,
no thinking hard of other things.
Blast it, I'd fly if I had wings
far, far away, I so hate this.
'Sahib, you go to Memsahib Browne?'
Now how did he ...? Well, put it down
to a sort of lucky guess, a miss
or hit, and for once it's been a hit.
'Yes, Bulaki. What of it?'

'Sahib, one thing only I vill speak.
When you are talking to Mem Browne
regard her nails.' Well, what a cheek!   He feels
How dare he tell me that. A frown   infuriated by
like monsoon thunder on his face,   the sergeant's
his temper boiling up apace,   interference.
he almost puts Ram on a charge.
Yet something stops him. Please enlarge
on your remark, he'd like to say.
He'd like to ask just what it meant.
Try as he may, he can't invent
any cunning white man's way
of asking. He turns on his heel.
The answer time may still reveal.

Then, before he's had a chance
to think once more what he will say,
she's there, Miss Browne. And, oh, her glance,
he feels, will shrivel all away
the least pale shoot that's in his mind
of any way to get behind
her cool exterior. He longs to mutter
some excuse. He feels an utter
fool. But then ... Then he does
what old Bulaki has suggested,
an idea he's not yet digested.
He gives her nails one glance. A buzz
of something straight away invades
his head. Gets stronger. Stronger. Fades.

But then that buzz becomes a thought,
a thought quite clear, as clear as gin,
as if a passing moth's been caught
and fixed on cork, held with a pin.
Her nails are slightly tinged with blue.
And now, Jack thinks, I have a clue
to something that ought not to be.
Jacqueline, he knows this, he
has been told it plain as plain,
always says she comes from Surrey,
her family's there. She says they worry
about her in the monsoon rain.
But blue in nails tells just one tale:
Indian blood, however pale.

However pale, however well
she's learnt her English – *blacky-white.*
A chi-chi. Though there's none to tell
in any other way, the sight
of those blued nails tells all.
Jack thinks I never can recall
ever having seen her nails
without a sheen of red. She fails   Under an English
to paint them just for once, and like   look he discovers
a kite Bulaki Ram swoops down.   an Anglo–Indian,
And puts the handcuffs on Miss Browne.   one beyond the pale.
Her secret out, though ladylike
no sahib will dare to ask her hand.
Instead, to bed no wedding-band.

So, what, Jack thinks, if somehow Milly
got to know. Did Jacqueline
visit her? Is that so silly?
Would she kill when it must mean
if she did not her secret's out?
No, wait. Just think. There was that shout,
that single cry of *No, Jack, no!*
She'd not be 'Jack' if this is so.
So Jacqueline is off the hook?
Relief came flooding through his mind.
Not now to have to pry behind
that cool disguise, that English look.
He managed then to ask if when
all were asleep one of the men ...

And Jacqueline said all the while
she'd slept, log-like, and if a soul
had walked about, or gone with guile
out from the Club, quiet as a mole,
she'd no idea who it might be.
'All I can say, it was not me.'
'Oh, no, of course, it wasn't you.
I just wondered ... hoped you knew.'
Jack beat retreat. Still felt a fool.
And yet, he thought as he went out,
poor woman. For without a doubt
if others guess she'll feel the cruel
hiss of gossip, gup, lap round.
And soon some fatal fault be found.

And here there comes again the call
of duty, all the shriller now
because Jack has discounted all
save one. It's one from seven. *How,*
though how, am I, Jack Steele, to go
to him? The Padre? Make friend foe?
Instead of seeking grave advice
I'll have to – What? Well, suffice
to say, a bad half-hour awaits.
To treat as known criminal,
no matter how subliminal,
a clergyman. It grates, it grates.
To put on my official pose.
That's rot, the whole world knows.

And yet, well, I suppose I must,
I can't do this as friend to friend.
But I thought I had his trust,
that he was one I could offend
and be forgiven, with a smile,
one who in the time of trial
I could rely on as a pal.
Is this the time when I shall
betray my friend, and with a pose?
Is there no other way for me?
Must I be stiff? Unbended knee,
my attitude? Oh, how it goes
against the grain. A hypocrite,
must that be the way of it?

Jack finds the Padre in his church
(he somehow feels that's not quite right).
Only after a long search
cast line secured fished-for bite.
Then, spotting in the dim interior
his friend – my spiritual superior? –
he asks himself why he should feel
it wrong to think a priest should kneel
before the altar. Surely that
is where a priest should best be found?
But Peter Fox? Although he's sound
as a bell, well still, his hat
is somehow not a saintly one.
It's rather just a hat for fun.

Till this minute that was not
something Jack had quite thought out.
But now he knows it. It is what
he's always felt. Something about
this friend of his is ... well, half-wrong.
All right, in church, when loud in song,
he seems a parson through and through.
But, once outside, he is a new
man, one who lacks just any trace   He compares
of holiness. What in fact   Padre and
the *sadhu* has he somehow lacked.   Indian
Jack registered this was the case,   holy man.
although perhaps it wasn't right
to compare a Black to White.

But he knows such thoughts as these
should not be aired, or even thought.
An English parson on his knees?
Well, there are some who might be caught
in private prayer. But Peter Fox?
He's no R.C. Confession box
is not his style. That death at noon?
If there's confessing, one who soon
may have to speak's the man inside
that cool church there. Once more
shoulders straight, go through the door.
'Peter, hello. Well, time and tide
have brought me here. I've got to ask –'
All along you've worn a mask?

Under that mask of cheery smiles
what lurks? And what on earth can I
say that will expose his wiles?
If wiles there are. If he's a lie.
But surely, surely, he is not.
He's what he seems. Not a jot
of evil's there. He go creeping
off to Milly, hot lust seeping
from every pore in noontide sweat?
No. 'Oh, Peter, just – well, just
to ask – No, listen, can I trust
you with a secret? I've not yet
told anyone I'm on the track
of who killed Milly. It's one Jack.'

'Jack? You mean you somehow know
her killer was a man called Jack?'
'Well, yes. A cry of *No, Jack, no!*
was heard and was reported back
to me. So, who it is I've got
to find – you know that there is not
a single Jack, except for me –
is someone who's a Jack, you see,
but not a Jack by given name.'
And now the Padre gives a smile.
'I'll tell you one who's not a mile
from here.' 'Yes? Who?' 'I'm not to blame.
But when I was a naval chaplain
they called me Jack, both crew and Captain.'

'But why? Your name, of course, is Peter.'
'Well, yes, it is. But then, you see ...
Jack Tar. You see, what could be neater
than call a Holy Joe like me
a Holy Jack.' 'But gosh. Well, gosh,
I mean to say – I know it's tosh
but, well, I've thought of everyone
who could have been the one who's done
that thing, and they – It's only you
who seems to have a Jack-like name.'
'So you are thinking I'm to blame?'
'Well, no. But then – but, well then, who?'
'What if I swear to God I'm not –'
He stopped. 'I'm sorry but I've got –'

A sort of smile. 'I'll re-phrase that.
If I'm to swear on something true,
if I should say not what comes pat,
as now I feel I'm bound to do,
then God is not who I must swear on.
I DON'T BELIEVE. Now, keep your hair on.
A clergyman who's made his vow?
Well, it's just so.' 'But, Peter, how
do you ... Well, what I want to know ...'
'How, although I don't believe, I still
can take a Service, say I will
do all I do? The status quo,
in short. Well, there it is, I do.
If you were me, well, wouldn't you?'

Jack thinks awhile. The church is cool,
silent too. Time passes. He,
though feeling pretty much a fool,
agrees that, yes, if it should be   Another case
he ever was in such a case,   of hypocrisy
well, rather than he'd lose all face   makes our
he might pretend he's what he's not.   hero think.
Then, though it's cool, he feels too hot.
Because from this odd unbeliever
will he get a true reply
if he asks: You did it, why?
He's, admitted, a deceiver.
But, if now I'm asked to trust,
well, can you trust a man in lust?

'I see your trouble, Jack, my friend,'
the unbelieving priest replies.
'I'd like to swear and put an end
to your dilemma. But it's lies
I fear you feel must surely come
from someone – Look, now you're a chum.
Just take my word. An Englishman's.'
Jack ponders. From a man who's sans
God, sans Church, sans everything?
Well, yes, he thinks, when all is done,
the Padre's still the sort that one
trusts because his ways all ring
with truth. A gentleman is what
he is. Enough. His word I've got.

PART SEVEN

Dismayed, disheartened, poor Jack Steele
now retires to lick his sores.　　　　　He reviews
How he'd hoped he would reveal　　　　his situation
the killer *Jack* at once. Because　　　　and assesses
he had to, the D.C. had said.　　　　　his progress.
The Station, he'd decreed, must shed
any taint from Milly's death,
any scandal, the least breath,
before next day when that M.P.
arrives to poke a prying nose
into anything that goes
astray in England's rule. If he
with one suspicious sniff discloses
that all here doesn't smell of roses ...

Is there yet time to put things right?
Have I neglected any task
that fell to me? Not thought quite
as hard I ought? Failed to ask
the single question, put it when
I should? My score? Nine out of ten.
Or at worst, say, eight I could
award myself. That fair? But should
I have somehow scored one more?
Have I failed to twist the bit
because of what it might have hit?
Somewhere have I failed to bore
that deeper inch because of what
I might have hit and wished I'd not?

Perhaps I did. Reduce that score.
Six out of ten? Well, if it's so,
was it too risky to score more?
Worse secrets there? Worse? Oh, no.
Surely they're still decent chaps.
Bar just that one. All would collapse
if truly rotten each one here
proves when souls are laid all bare.
Already Jack had seen enough
not as he'd thought. Carter found
a deviant. The Padre, sound
though he was, his faith a bluff.
Arthur Brent, in tell-tale funk?
The Surgeon, self-confessed a drunk.

Once more, next day, Jack goes to see
F.H.R. How much he longs
to find – a miracle – that he
is on his feet, that all the wrongs
will in an hour be turned to rights.
A thought that warms him and delights.
Gone any thought of glory snatched
from deepest mire. He knows he's matched
himself against much more than he
can battle with. Now he is willing
to pass the baton. Milly's killing
weighs so hard that it must be
a task that with no sense of loss
he can hand over to his boss.

For stink, Jack knows, there's bound to be.
He's learnt a murder such as this
means secrets no one ought to see
will to the light, by hit or miss,
be brought implacably. That all,
or nearly all, the sins – the fall
from grace, the weakness hidden still,
the living lie – that all such will
as the probe is slowly turned
come squirming up. And one man then
must see them, weigh them, and say when
the wickednesses he's discerned
may be put back into the dark.
Or be held out, and let dogs bark.

But no sooner had Jack stepped
into the ward than there he saw
– he almost felt he could have wept –
Guthrie was quite clearly more
in danger than, it seemed, he'd been
the day before. The sickly sheen
on forehead, chest, revealed it all.
Here was a man you could not call
on for help beyond what he
might mutter out of gummy lips.
And even such might well be tips
as wrong as tipster's given free.
'Well, lad, who was it? I suppose
by now the whole damn Station knows.'

'Well, no, sir. I did as you said
and talked my best to each of those
who, when poor Milly was left dead
slept at the Club –' 'Sweet repose,'
the sick man shouted loud and clear.
Oh God, Jack thought, is his time near?
Delirious, that's the only word.
Help from him? Absurd. Absurd.
It well could be within a day
I'll once more stand beside a grave.
Ask one thing more, he'll only rave.
'Look, sir, I've only come to say
I hope you're better soon.' He went,
gripped by yet deeper discontent.

Oh, yes, it's up to me, he thought.
I had my hopes. Now they're all dead.
And well I know just what I ought
to do. But how? It's me instead
of Guthrie. I've already failed.
My colours to the mast I nailed.
But rank life has shot them down.
It needs a hero, not a clown.
A hero who can toss aside
whatever foulness he might find,
dive and re-surface, all unlined
by any evil found inside
the cesspit that I fear I saw
when I began to peek and pore.

Jack spent the day, a useless round,
in seeing each of those he'd seen
and asking, like a scentless hound,
questions that had too well been
answered. First to Mr Wright.
'Corbyn M.P. comes here tonight.'
Then to the Surgeon. 'Oh, go away,
I've better things to do today.'
To the Padre. 'Jack, I've told
you everything.' Next Plum Duff.
'Look, lad, I know it's tough ...'
To Jacqueline, still icy cold,
for all he knows what she yet hides.
One moment, while suspicion rides,

he asks himself: what if now I
accuse her, not of Milly's murder
but of lying. Ask her why
she acts like one who's safe in purdah,
pretends she lives without a worry,
claims she's a miss from prudish Surrey,
when all the while her nails proclaim
Chillicracker her real name.
Yes, tell that though her skin is pale
black native blood runs in her veins.
She'd weep, however much she feigns
a cool indifference. Tear the veil,
then what would come to light of day?
Something? In my searchlight ray?

Then like a horse brought to a check
he brings his thoughts, so runaway,
to a sharp halt. Now wait a sec,
just what it is I'm on the way
to think of here? I was about
to relish what, without a doubt,
I could now do. To punish her
not for a fault but cause a stir
in telling all just so I'd see
a woman squirm as if a lash ...
as if I was a man to thrash
a quaking girl. And that – that's me?
Deep down within am I one such?
Pitch lies there, and will I touch?

Jack pulls himself together now.
I cannot sit for ever here.
Slime-sucked feet must leave the slough
though I would wallow in despair.
Murder or not, routine awaits.
If Guthrie's for the pearly gates
(for him at once they'll swing apart)
before they send his counterpart
I must make sure all's well in order.
Each crime reported put in hand,
no paper left unfiled. Oh, and
check the gaol to the last warder.
So to the *daftar* Jack Steele goes,
determined to keep on his toes.

Outside, Bulaki Ram salutes.
'Sahib, D.C. is vanting you.'
Jack's heart – it's barely left his boots –   Hearing he's
sinks swiftly back. Now, what's to do?   been summoned
To see him, yes. But what's it mean?   by the great
I've seen him. Heck, it's only been   man he panics.
two hours at most since we last met.
What can he want? Is it a threat?
Or – can it be? – a word of praise?
No, I've done nothing that deserves
praise at all as yet. My nerves
are, frankly, all upset. A daze
of worry. Well, dispel it right
away and on the bullet, bite.

Bulaki comes up at a run
as Jack proceeds along his way.
'Sahib, Wright Sahib is Number One.'
'I don't need –' No, let him say
what he wants. He's well-meant.
I depend to some extent
on the fellow. Let him chatter.
What he says can't really matter,
whatever gup he wants to spew.
'Yes, sahib, my older cousin-brother
tells Wright Sahib was like no other
when first he came. Sahib, this is true.
What he was doing once at night –'
What is this? Some jet of spite?

What is the fellow ...? No, but still,
I shouldn't tell him to pipe down,
there's lots of things that if he will
he'd do for me. Try not to frown
while like this he gabbles on,
although I wish that he was gone.
I want to try and think just what
Mr Wright may want, and not
to listen to this jabber-jab.
What's this now? Wright Sahib once
pinned a thief ...? He heard his grunts.
Pinned him down before he'd grab
the watch he'd put beneath his head?
His jack-knife through right to the bed?

'Sahib, in those days long ago
Wright Sahib they always used to name
as Jack-knife Sahib. Did you know?'
What is this? Is this the same
man, our very own D.C.?
I didn't know, but it must be.
Jack-knife Sahib. And if that's so
– Mr Wright? And sunk so low? –
what more likely he's called Jack
sometimes by those he's known for long.
And, worse, unless I've got it wrong
Milly and Mike he knew way back.
So now what is it I must do?
See if his footprint fits the shoe.

Bulaki Ram has dropped behind.
For just a bit Jack thinks of him.
What did the fellow have in mind
telling me ...? No, he's too dim.
But now again his thoughts he turns
to Mr Wright. But what churns
inside his head is not just what
the D.C. might want. It's not
that at all. It's how on earth
he can mention that jack-knife.
Derek Wright has got a wife.   Abruptly he
All right, she's subject of some mirth,   looks ahead to
but nonetheless she's not to cross.   what may face him
He may be D.C., she's the boss.   at the worst.

Jack thinks then: Oh God, what if
I challenge him and he confesses.
I'd have to then – hell, this is stiff –
arrest him. I've been in some messes
while out here, felt Guthrie's tongue,
been made to feel I was a young
good-for-nothing. But – but this
surely is the end. What bliss
to find I'm dreaming, but, oh, no,
I'm not. It's real. I've got to face
the D.C., ask *Is it the case*
you were called Jack-knife long ago?
He answers yes, and after that
You're Jack? Into the fire, the fat.

'Ah, Steele, I asked you to come back
because I've had a second thought' –
Hell with that. It's *Are you Jack?*
that's what. And then the court? –
'about how we should treat the matter
of Milly's death.' All this patter
when I have only got to say
Are you Jack? Then stag at bay?
A struggle next, a test of wills?
And if I win ...? 'I think, you know,
it's better if we make a show
of honesty. It's truth that kills
suspicions that there's worse behind.
I'm sure that you're much of my mind.'

What is this he's asking me?
If I, Jack Steele, just out of school,
after due thought, do I agree
he's found the only way to fool
this M.P. whose too-sudden visit
could be trouble? Well, think. Is it?
No, it's not. *To make a show*?
An M.P.'s sharp. He's bound to know
we haven't told him all the facts.
But, worse: will there be now to tell
that our D.C.'s bound for a cell?
And is that why like this ... he acts?
Is he afraid? And so should I
ask *Did you, Jack, see Milly die?*

Jack baulks at it. Some things there are
he cannot do. He cannot try
to topple gods. They are too far
above. He asks: Oh, who am I
to challenge Mr Wright or any
such? F.H.R.? Among the many
I've been taught I should revere,
been taught indeed to hold in fear?
The head at school. Even the King.
They're the ones who always know
what to do and where to go.
They always do the decent thing.
'Yes, sir,' he answers. 'Yes, you're right.
You want me to explain tonight?'

'Why, yes. Good man. The fact, quite bare.
And our M.P. can whistle then
for any more. Or, well, look here,
say Milly met her death just when
we had trouble in the town.
Let him think that, and put it down
to dacoits, with us on their scent.'
Jack gulped the pill. And then he went.   He agrees
Dejection rose, a choking mist.   to deceive
To tell the truth yet add a lie?   the awkward
Is that how those who sit on high   visitor.
run things? But then the rod I've kissed.
I have agreed. The truth I'll smother.
But worse, far worse, there is that other.

The question that I failed to put.
I failed to ask the D.C. god
if Jack-knife Sahib at his bed's foot
once pinned a thief (still in quod?),
and was as ruthless when it came
to Milly, hiding then his shame?
Did he see her, too, as a threat?
Did Jack-knife see each of them get
come-uppance at his iron-willed hand?
Yet young and simple as I am,
at least I did see through that sham.
Now, at least I understand
that even men straight as a die
will in stress tell blackest lie.

Because for all which Jack has lacked
in courage, there's one thing he's gained
(if gain it is, he thinks, guilt-racked).
At last he has, though shocked and pained,
begun to learn that what's above
is not always hand in glove
with what's below. A fissured gap
– the lesson's hard for any chap –
he's learnt most often lies between
a surface smooth, unbroken crust,
quite safe to tread on, fit to trust,
and turmoil seething there unseen
by eyes that try not to look deep
or only risk the swiftest peep.

PART EIGHT

'Mr Steele, once more, well done.'
Jack shook the M.P.'s outstretched hand.   His own lie told,
'The hunt is really well begun,   he submits to
or so at least I understand.   undeserved praise.
Hard on the trail – now, am I right? –
of those thieves – by day? by night? –
who killed that lady in her bed.
The cowards who killed her and then fled.
Good work, say I.' 'When duty calls
all one can do is do one's best.'
What have I said? If I confessed ...
Dacoits he means. Oh, God, what balls.
And I must say that's what I think?
'Yes, sir. Dacoits, flushed with drink.'

Jesus, what's this stuff I'm adding
to the fairytale we're telling?
Making dacoits drunk? What padding.
And now I know that we are selling
him a lie just to preserve
an image that we don't deserve,
a fact that just today I've found.
Not what we seem. A four-pound
note. That is what I see us as.
Why don't – Who is that pretty girl?
And, in a moment, in a whirl
of dancing steps the creature has
come up to where with the M.P.
Jack stands. Whoever can this be?

'Mr Steele, this is my niece,'
the M.P. says. 'She seems intent
on meeting you. I'll get no peace –'
'I'm Jessica,' she says, hell-bent
it seems on cutting through convention.
Her uncle laughs. 'My good intention
overtaken, something I
am getting used to. Although why
I let you jump the gun I never
know, my dear.' At that she grins.
He sighs. 'Well, it is for my sins,
since I agreed to bring my clever
niece along, on board the ship,
and now on my fact-finding trip.'

'Well, Uncle, you won't find out much
unless I'm there to prick a pin
in what you're told. It's Double Dutch
you swallow just like Bombay gin.'
'Now, Jessica, that's just not true.'
'It isn't? Right then, tell me who
you were talking with just now.'
'The D.C., dear.' 'A sacred cow.'
'Jessica, now watch your tongue.'
'No. Isn't that the right word here
for a panjandrum, made to fear?'
'Well, cows are sacred,' answers young
Jack. 'And, yes, true, no one will
challenge them for good or ill.'

'Okay, I think you've made my case.
Your D.C., whatever he may say
goes out as truth. The ruling race
has spoken. Grovel, kneel, obey.'
Jack manages to give a laugh,
though inwardly he thinks that half
what she has said is all too true.
Half? Well, more in his view.
But, no, he's not just now about
to say aloud that she is right.
Specially when he sees – a kite –
the D.C. swooping down. To rout
this very cheeky pretty minx?
I'll defend her, Jack Steele thinks.

But then at once he knows that he
won't dare to. He is here for years
to come, while she, a gadfly, she
will go within a day. No tears
for her from god-like wrath. She'll go.
Did her *pins* hurt? She'll never know.
'Mr Corbyn, here's a thought.
Our cinema has just now bought,
I understand, the bran-new reels
of the King-Emperor's Jubilee
flown out from London. Did you see
them? Is that something that appeals?'
'I did see them –' 'Oh, Uncle, I
never did. I thought I'd cry.

Come with me, do. A second view
won't harm you, Uncle.' Shake of head.
'It's just tonight?' 'Yes, sir, if you
would like to go,' the D.C. said,
'I'll see they keep you a good seat.'
'Well, sorry, I'm afraid this heat
has done for me. I must to bed.'
'Look, can't you go with me instead?'
Jessica now looks straight at Jack.
He'd like to take the offer up,
to risk Club gossips with their gup.
But, he thinks, it will look black
if Steele, intrepid dacoit-taker,
is seen as just a poodle-faker.

'Alas, I can't. I am on duty,'
Jack says. Or those the words he speaks.
But what's conveyed. *Oh, you beauty.*
Wouldn't I just ... And that's what leaks.
Young Jessica's a cunning piece.
'Mr Wright, I'm sure the police
come under you. Won't you tell
this nice young man he's got to quell,
for just this once, that stiff unbending
attitude? Can't he relax
for just an hour?' And now all Jack's
hopes go springing up. Unending
bliss he doesn't see. But he
sees, and wants, one hour that's free.

An hour, or two, when he can be
the boy he was, not long ago.
A boy, eighteen, and fancy free.
Time then ran fast that now goes slow,
each minute burdened by that task,
the questions that he's feared to ask.
The D.C. smiles. A pretty girl
can set a locked-up heart a-whirl.
'Yes, Steele,' he says, 'it's not my beat,
but off you go. You'll be the better
for a break and – well, you may net a
dacoit on your way.' A feat,
Jack thought with hidden rage, that's more
unlikely than a snake will roar.

But now away goes all his fret.
He'd been told, an order stated,
to escort this pretty pet.
To go with her on a belated
trip to town, such as it was.
His heart leapt up, not just because
a break from his too weighty load
had come. But who had put the goad
to Mr Wright? Just her. Then doubt.
Mr Wright, he is the cloud
that shadows me. Have I allowed
the ruthlessness that once leapt out
to be forgot? Is he that Jack
both now and all those long years back?

Wright sahib has he been quick to see
a chance to keep pursuit away?
Let this young chap, as off goes he,
forget the hunt, think what we say
is what's the truth, believe the tale,
forget the facts, and into gaol
put some black dacoit he may find.
A useful sham, leave truth behind.
Abandon now his ceaseless quest,
and, once this M.P.'s visit's done,
see Milly's death as simply one
that can be left, or time may wrest
at some far day the hidden truth.
He rates me then a colt uncouth?

Two hours ago (although by now
in an *ekka* they both sat)
Jack almost faced the sacred cow,
told him what he had thought that
he, this god of his, had done.
A moment like when with his gun
he'd faced that tusker, fired and killed.
But, no, it needed one more skilled.
If Guthrie sahib, that stricken knight ...
'Drive on.' The driver flicks his whip.
Soon Jack is revelling in the trip.
A pretty girl. The Indian night.
Seize the day. There is tomorrow.
Seize on joy, to hell all sorrow.

'Thank God,' she says, 'we're out of that.'
'Out of what?' 'That ghastly Club.'
'Ghastly? But it's where we chat
and take our ease, just like a pub
where natives are ten thousand miles
away, where jokes bring only smiles,
not looks around in case we see
spying eyes who hope that we
are saying what will cast a shade
on King, on Emperor, and on us.'
'Oh, really, Jack, how you do fuss.
You sound to me like some old maid.
Or, worse, you're acting the White Man.
You're acting, acting hard as you can.'

'I'm acting? No, that isn't so.'
'Oh, Jack, think. Just look at you.
Boiled shirt, black tie in a neat bow,
dinner jacket. How you stew
on such a sultry Indian night.'
He bridled. 'Well, but – well, all right,
do you think we should dine dirty?'
'*Dine dirty.* Listen, don't get shirty
but can't you hear how very wrong
that sounds? My God, what tommyrot.'
Jack feels she's put him in a spot.
A bird, somewhere, breaks into song,
a did-you-do-it. Can I, thought Jack,
tell her its name and so get back?

Get back to where we were? That's out.
Did you do it? In a second
she'd be asking all about
our murder case. That Milly beckoned
and how males went flocking there:
something she must never hear.
Yes, she's so direct I think
I'd fail to hide – well, yes, I shrink
from anything that might expose
that lie that I agreed to tell.
Forget that bird, and hope all's well.
Except she thinks – well, I suppose
that I and all the rest out here,
just play a game, and out of fear.

The cinema. Not quite like Home.
No Odeon, no picture palace,
no Wurlitzer, no gilded dome.
It's through the looking-glass with Alice:
the whole scene somehow upside-down.
Rich in the front, and then the brown,
the poor, are pushed right to the back.
'For us? Those cane chairs? Really, Jack?'
'But, yes.' He smiled. 'And we must play
our parts. That's something that's expected.'
He glanced at her and then detected
a little grin, as much to say,
Ah, well, I can't keep up my pique.
So now it's *Pax.* A narrow squeak.

The lights go down and on the screen
flickers the title they're to see.
The Swashbuckler and – a scene
from it comes back to Jack – *Kali.*
No, *the Evil Kali.* Years
ago he saw this film. Wild cheers
at school, all clapped and lapped it up.
The hero, white-clad. In close-up
never showing fright or fear.
The evil goddess hung with skulls.
Action. Courage. It never dulls
in his imagination where
men are men, and Evil lies
beneath the sun-smote Indian skies.

'India? Come, it's not like that?'
Jessica asks when it's all done.
'Well, no. No, a caveat
I'll enter there. That was just fun.
And India, yes, it's otherwise.
Evil's more complex. Not all lies
lie in those wearing native dress,
I have just now begun to guess.'
'You're managing to get on top
of what you're told? Now, do you see
things are not what they seem to be
in that world you call your shop?'
She's gone too far. Jack feels a spurt
of anger. Does she think we're dirt?

How can she leave out of account
all the good it is we do?
All the problems we surmount
that over years just grew and grew
with no one with the guts to act?
Does she not know there's a compact
which England ever keeps as true,
although there were not any who
on India's side could offer us
any gift worth half as much?
Has she seen that there are such
men as Arthur Brent? No fuss,
but under him the roads get built.
How can she say we should feel guilt?

But guilt is what she seems to think
we ought to feel, and just because
some starve while we have food and drink.
When we weren't here the country was
in turmoil. Then the men who knew
how to rule, who dared say boo
to wicked geese, came to the land
with Law and Order. Understand
that and then it's plain to see
that Derek Wright and others such
are gifts from God, that their touch
is magic, that when two or three
like him are dropped into the welter
there's justice, order, peace and shelter.

Yes, even someone soaked in drink
like Dr Prosser. He brings sense,
Western science link by link
built up for centuries. Then pretence
and mumbo-jumbo slink away
(or I'm sure they will one day).
And Edward Carter, making grow
two stalks where one or none would go
before. Yes, there's another doing good.
Plum Duff, too, he keeps alive
poems that would not live and thrive.
And most of all, one that I should
have put as first, yes, F.H.R.,
dread of the wicked near and far.

Jack finds he cannot say out loud
all that he feels about his heroes.
Then, driving back, a rain-thick cloud
adds dark to night, swift as zeroes
added on to 10, at one a minute.
At any second they'll begin it,
those clouds, he thinks. And then my first
monsoon will break. It's true, I thirst
to feel its rain that in the past
I've heard and read so much about.
I'll feel that then I have *come out.*
A youth no more, I'll be at last
presented at a Drawing Room.
Far off, a threat, a thunder boom.

But then as through the dark they ride,
looking back a fearful thought
breaks in on Jack. Should all that pride
he cherished then be set at naught
by what he, bumbling, has found out?
In every hero there's a doubt?
Always a worm within the rose?
My killer must be one of those
I was all set to put before
this girl as fine. He wants to speak.
Say something. Show he's not been weak.
He draws a breath. But then downpour.
Yes, the monsoon. Here. The air
is water, liquid, blast and blare.

The *ekka* halts. Driver and horse
battered into statues where
they stand. The road a watercourse,
almost a river. But then, near,
Jack spots, dark though it is, a hut.
He seizes Jess – no if, no but –
and pushes her through all the rain
towards the black shape, might and main.
What if, he thinks, inside the place
we find there are a pack of thieves?
But the situation leaves
no other course. It is a race
between soaked skin or roof of sorts.
Above, the thunder's loud reports.

Waterproof or not, the hut
smells of spices, human sweat.
From time to time its dark is cut
by lightning flashes. But the wet,
it seems, at least is kept at bay.
'Are you all right?' Jack thinks to say.
'Well, yes. Yes, I think I am,'
she answers. And then, 'Oh, damn,
I'm in a mess. I think that I
have trodden in some frightful goo.
I think it's leaked into my shoe.'
Another flash. And in Jack's eye
a photo of a stork-legged girl
toppling in a giddy whirl.

He leaps, arms out, and catches her.
They're nearly down. He holds her tight.
Holds tight, and feels the hot blood stir.
Inside the hut it's double night.
And she? Clasped hard in his embrace?
He feels – he's sure – at least a trace
of answering blood, like his astir.
He presses more. There's no demur.
A kiss. Deep, warm, the blood alight
by body pressed to body hard.
Long-nurtured rules all but unbarred.
But then another flash, pin-bright,
and crouched there like a cornered rat
Jack sees two eyes. And all goes flat.

And now Jack hears the gossip spread.
The police sahib and an English miss
doing it, and not in bed.
Shameless, a whore. A precipice
before him yawns, the natives' laughter.
That is what all sahibs are after.
Yet ... Oh, yet is it so wrong?
From her to me I felt that strong
current passing to and fro.
I know that we have scarcely met,
but sometimes surely ... Yet ... Ah, yet ...
But, no. And I've been taught that's so.
Marriage plans must not be counted
until a fellow's properly mounted.

Oh, yes, it all comes down to this:
one's pay is such, a horse is dear.
No question then of married bliss
without a pony and its gear.
Jack stands there now as turned to stone.
She beside him. But alone,
each one. That crouching shape a threat
to cool all ardour. Now the wet
penetrates the hut's thin thatch.
Great drops of water strike Jack's head.
He peers outside. And, yes, instead
of inky night a lighter patch.
'Let's go,' Jack says. 'It can't be worse
out there than here.' He wants to curse.

He wants to swear and shout and kick.
It's all gone wrong, his hour of grace
from duty's call. Yes, now the tick
of time he hears, apace, apace,
knows once more he's failed to find
that other Jack, the one behind
dead Milly's murder. Now once more
that whole conundrum, sharp and raw,
comes stalking back into his mind.
Jack! No, Jack! Once more that yell.
Once more he hears the *chhokra* tell
his tale. If tale that single blind
cry can still be called. It can.
It points, a signpost, at one man.

Through the ever-pouring rain,
if slacker now than once it was,
the *ekka* plods, on slackened rein.
Jack feels he ought (to be no dunce)
to talk, if only making chat.
'Well,' he says, 'there's something that
came out of all this evening's mess.
At least you saw the film that, yes,
you'd said you'd missed, the Jubilee.'
Beside him in the dark she laughed.
'That film? Now, Jack, don't be so daft.
Just my excuse. Who'd want to see
it more than once, that rigmarole.'
Rigmarole? That takes its toll.

Jack feels a sullen sense of shock.
Himself, he'd frankly revelled in
the power, the glory, both a rock
to cling to in a world of sin.
The King, from all his earliest days
he'd learnt to reverence the ways
of royalty. *God Save the King,*
the words, the tune. If anything
went darting to his inner core
it was the feeling that arose
each time, yes, heaven knows,
those words he heard. Or even saw
a picture of the King. But now
this girl had scorned that long-held vow.

PART NINE

At last to bed. A silent ride
Jack had endured after that shock.
He could not chatter when his pride   _{Failing to gain}
had been so undermined, made mock   _{feminine}
of by a girl whom he'd begun   _{consolation, he}
to feel – what those few hours had done – _{sinks into gloom.}
might come to be ... *No, it's clear,*
no lady-killer me, I fear.
And then the day. The stealthy shave,
still half-asleep. His clothes laid out.
His morning ride, if spoilt by doubt.
At last reluctantly he gave
his daily orders. Now to see
if F.H.R. can still help me.

He found him worse, or quite as bad
as he had been the day before.
His moans, like one gone truly mad,
in burst on burst, both quick and raw,
put in Jack's mind (so often heard)
the sound of the brain-fever bird.
And, when he rose from that blind pit,
even worse the words that it
sent spewing from those once-stiff lips.
Bilge of sex so graphic that
Jack blushed and felt the slime go splat
into his face. The rant of whips,
of whores, of acts half-understood.
Jack would have left then if he could.

But, worse for him, while Guthrie raved
the Matron entered and stood by.
Jack thought a woman should be saved
from filth like this. 'Oh, Matron, I
feel you'd better block your ears.'
'Young man, do you think in my years
in hospitals I've not heard worse?
Men's minds are sinks. Not one's averse
to swilling in his head such stuff.'
Jack feels he's had another shock.
All he is learning, like a flock
of evil birds. It's not enough
that Jessica has rocked his trust,
now he's told how wide goes lust.

'The King, the King,' sick Guthrie shouts.
Jack winces. Guthrie joining now
with Jessica in hurling doubts
at England's King? He wonders how
if Guthrie does at last get well
he'll face him. Then another yell.
'The Queen, the Queen, the Knave, the Jack.'
This is *Hamlet*? Jack goes back
to odd bits Guthrie sometimes utters.
But one thing's sure, he thinks, I'll not
get any help from him if what
he shouts is all this stuff. The gutters
frothing filth, and spilling, spouting.
All my cherished faith he's flouting.

Jack leaves without another word,
and outside finds the Surgeon waiting.
'Well, young man?' Then, undeterred
by alcoholic breath, just stating
what's in his mind Jack answers up.
'Doctor, he'll die?' 'Oh, no, you pup.
You think I'm not in any state
to find a treatment till too late?
Want me to tell you what I fear?
It's not the sun. But typhus may
present his symptoms. I won't say
it's that –' A laugh. 'But, well, how queer
if a chap like him from just
one lousy louse-bite bites the dust.'

Soaking soon in monsoon rain
– and in despair – Jack thinks of how
his hero, thanks to blotting pain,
is a hero no more now.
His forceful mind is shown to hide
foul thoughts, black lusts, all there inside.
Jack thinks, too, of a hope he'd nursed
that when at last the monsoon burst,
its sudden cool, its sweet relief,
would bring his answer like a gift.
That when clouds came his cloud would lift.
But nothing had. Who like a thief
had crept to be a lady killer
still lost in cloud. No fiery pillar.

Nor could he see a single way
to add to what he had found out.
He could – once more into the fray –
ask again, a clumsy lout,
the questions he'd had on his list.
But he well knows there is no twist
he can invent to give a hope
of finding under microscope
the tiniest something clear and new.
In the *daftar* by his chair
he finds Bulaki standing there.
Scarcely knowing why, he drew
up another chair, said 'Sit,'
and told his troubles bit by bit.

Some he concealed or hinted at,
no more. And not a word, of course,
about that hut, what there was that
happened there. His dull remorse
saw to that. But he gave vent
to all he felt with Guthrie spent
as a force to urge him on.
Nothing, though, to hint that gone
was the respect that once had been.
But he felt he just might tell
how Guthrie raved, was far from well.
'He shouts out *King and Knave and Queen*.
I think it is some English play
that's in his head. Why I can't say.'

'Oh, sahib,' Bulaki then breaks in,
raja and *rani* is reminding.'
He gives that Indian wag of chin.
'All that mess that we were finding
in Marchbanks bungalow.
Steele sahib, do you want I go,
do level best to put same right?'
Jack waves him off. He thinks: no light
of course from him. I was a fool
to hope to get some good idea
from a native, to make clear,
the way a master might at school
explain a tricky bit of Greek.
Oh Christ, I've shown myself so weak.

An hour went by. Jack just sat there.
He lacked the will to stir at all.
But then Bulaki's once more here.
'Sahib, job done. But one just small
thing I'm finding is nowhere.'
Jack scarcely heard. Well, do I care
what he has found or not? '*Thik hai.*'
That's fine. Or, may be not. Oh, why
am I here? Should I resign?
Go crawling Home? Do what? Sell cars?
Get roaring drunk to hide my scars?
To think I thought that here I'd shine.
'Sahib, is missing from her pack
one card. *Tash ka gulam*, jack.'

A bombshell here, and Jack jumped up.
'You say that all the cards he threw –'
So, not Jack. The lip and cup,
betwixt the two ... 'I think that you
may have hit, unwittingly,
on my mistake. Yes, you see,
if Milly's shout of *Jack! No jack!*
was because – Well, just think back.
A Patience game, and then she finds
a jack is missing. Well, her rage ...
They always said none could assuage ...'
He stops. High time that he reminds
himself there is a native here.
I said too much ...? My foot, a snare.

But it seems his *havildar*
has failed to follow all he's said.
There he stands, his gaze afar.
Not a thought there in his head.
Jack thinks: what's next for me to do?
Yes, to check. I'll listen to
that boy again. 'Bring him *ek dum*,'
he says. '*Jee*, sahib.' Well, not so dumb.
He's grasped the *chhokra*'s who I need.
Bulaki goes. Ten minutes pass
(Jack sits fuming, ants in arse).
The boy is brought. You'd think that he'd
in those few days become yet thinner.
What if ...? Jack thinks. Then I'm no winner.

What if – he hardly looks alive –
what if he can no longer do
that single trick that somehow I've
relied upon? Well, then my clue,
my only clue, has slipped away,
monsoon water, just a spray
left for a moment near a crack.
The *chhokra*, timid, looks at Jack.
'*Bolo,*' Bulaki tells the lad.
He lifts his head. It then droops low.
Oh God, Jack prays, it can't be so.
It's not. At last the sound that had
reverberated forth and back
in Jack's head. 'No jack! No jack!'

At once it's plain as plain can be
that Milly then was calling out
in fury when ... yes, clearly she
had just found out. Her angry shout.
A Patience pack in which by chance
a jack is lost. A merry dance
she'd lead her servant if she'd guessed
his the fault, or he confessed
he might have put the cards away
without, as ordered, counting through
the pack till he'd reached 52.
Jack gives the boy – he's earned his pay –
a whole rupee (in England less
than twenty pennies). It's largesse.

Bulaki when the boy had left
stood looking at the monsoon rain.
He murmurs, too, like one bereft
of reason. Is the fellow quite insane,
Jack asks himself, he really seems so.
These Indians, they always dream so.
No wonder they get nothing done.
A tusker to kill, it's mine the gun.
For now – how changed in half an hour –
he's full of energy and feels
the killer's soon laid by the heels.
Somehow. All it needs: willpower.
Bulaki mutters, 'Take *ek* card.'
Jack needs to think, but finds it hard.

And Bulaki's muttering still.
'In bungalow' and '*Kya* time?'
Jack snaps at him, his voice shrill,
'What time? The time when the crime ...?'
Why, noon, of course. But, no. Not then.
Milly was playing Patience when
the *chhokra* heard her make that row.
So ... 'Bulaki, pay attention now.
I'll tell you what's occurred to me.
The murder did not come at noon.
We fixed the time at much too soon.
She must have died – don't you agree? –
after the tennis tournament.
Yes, that's the time I must have meant.'

Good God, who am I talking to?
I thought – I'm dazed – it was some pal.
I hope Bulaki ... Wouldn't do ...   Confused by
A native. Oh, I see I shall   all he has
have to watch my tongue, or find   learnt, he reaches
he thinks that he's the one behind   back to former
all that I, a white man, do.   certainties.
So, stop it. He's not someone who
I could confide in, no, not I.
Now, pull yourself together, Jack.
Think hard, now you've got the knack.
What does this shift of time imply?
Yes, this. That I must look about
for some sahib who *then* went out.

Let me think. It must have been
during the match that afternoon.
Someone then who left the scene?
Yes, then abouts. Or maybe soon
after when, there in the bar,
I was the victor, F.H.R.
the loser, curious though that was.
Though, since, I've thought it was because
he had in mind a sticky task,
that elephant that we had heard
had gone beserk. That may have blurred
his concentration. I must ask
when he once more is on the mend.
Unless – Oh, God – he meets his end.

That's if Dr Prosser's right,
and he's got typhus. Then, if so,
tomorrow I may see the sight
of one more solemn graveyard show.
Though I believe for F.H.R.
real sorrow will be what they are
feeling as the coffin sinks.
With Milly, otherwise methinks.
As if in echo of those thoughts
Bulaki now says, 'Sahib, vat luck
if Guthrie sahib, now so sunstruck,
from *charpoy* in one sec reports
for duty. Then I think he vill
tell us who it is who kill.'

Jack grunted. 'Well, I hardly think
that Guthrie sahib, however tough,
will leave his bed all in a blink.
I told you: he was pretty rough.'
'Yes, sahib, sunstroke very bad.
vat I asking is: he had,
or no, his topee on?' And then ...
Then Jack recalls advice that when
one day his boss was teaching him
he took great pains to hammer home.
Outdoors a chap must never roam
without a hat, or not till dim
light at dusk allows him to.
So how had Guthrie gone askew?

Or rather *why*? Yes, why was he
out in the sun? Now Jack recalls
how F.H.R. so suddenly
had left the Club. The thought appals.
Could it be? Yes, can it be?
Could it really be that he,
the one man that had been his guide
to India, who in proper pride
had seemed to be Great Britain's best,
was – was the one who in the sun
had gone to Milly and had done
that awful deed? *His* thumbs had pressed
into her neck? And, worse, before
he'd gone to Milly as a whore?

Bulaki still is standing there.
Has he any inkling what
is on my mind? No, I swear
that one like him, well, just cannot
imagine that a sahib could hold
thoughts in his head so foully bold.
'Sir,' Bulaki says just then,
his voice uncertain once again,
'I have been hearing vat I vish
I never heard. Sir, vicked things.
Sir, a boy's here who mudslings
against out boss. Sir, most hellish.
A ward-boy, sir, at ho'pital.
Sir, he must be drown in spittle.'

'What on earth – out with it now.
What is all this? Some ward-boy's gup?'
'Sahib, he is telling, always, how
in ho'pital our boss jumps up
and shouts out many fearful thing
he to woman, sahib, with his ding
would like to do, or vat he did
in Angrezland and kept much hid.'
Jack realised that his hope was vain
that Guthrie's ravings could be quenched.
With all his strength he wrenched and wrenched
that foul-mouth scene, that once again
came back to him, out from his mind.
But nothing now could keep him blind.

No, the truth he must concede.
Guthrie, like a flame-sucked moth,
to Milly went in sexual greed.
And if she taunted, then his wrath
could well have leapt out like a bolt
of lightning, yes, a million-volt
discharge. And Milly's tender neck
worth no more than an unpaid cheque.
So Motive, yes. And Means, the vent
of rage in clawing hands. The third?
It's Opportunity. Absurd
not to see that Guthrie meant
to lose that tennis match and, too,
that he had made his rendezvous.

No wonder that with unspent lust
he went, without his topee on,
leaving her dead. I think he must
have walked and walked while hot sun shone
down upon his tortured frame.
Tortured? Yes, by sudden shame.
Because, and no mistaking here,
he was a man that all held dear.
Oh, yes, although it's almost sure
he is in fact that lady killer
I had to find. And now a chiller
thought strikes home. Though he's a poor
deluded man, and wicked, still
he's one I thought could do no ill.

PART TEN

Then came doubt. Could this be right?
Despite the way things came together,
perhaps seen in some other light
there'd be something to hint that, whether
all he'd heard and guessed was true
or not, there was another one who
also fitted this black bill.
Another one who'd had to kill.
No, what I want is final proof.
I may be caught in my own trap –
'Bulaki?' Damn, where is the chap?
The way he holds himself aloof.
Why can't he tell me something more?
For my trap, find a trap-door?

Jack looks about. Outside, the rain
has for the moment slackened off,
though water's gurgling down a drain.
Inside, no sound. No, not a cough.
Bulaki's gone, quiet as a ghost.
Just when, Jack thinks, I need him most.
He looks again and spots him now,
mooching along, a placid cow.
Now why has he deserted me
just when I thought I had arrived?
It's odd. I feel I've been deprived
of what I need. A shady tree,
a mounting block, a helping hand.
Quite why I cannot understand.

But, with him here or with him gone,
I must make up my mind for sure.
Brace up, brace up, my son John.
Do your duty. Kill or cure.
I must. I must. No help I need.
Bulaki? He's a broken reed.
What I must do to make all clear
is go to Guthrie, sink my fear.
Yes, I must ask him face to face
if it is he who murdered her.
You killed Milly? Answer, sir,
then know it's triumph or disgrace.
Jack stands. There is a mirror there.
Sam Browne adjusted. Comb to hair.

He takes the *daftar* bicycle.
At least, he thinks, the way's quite long.
Because chill dread, cold as an icicle,
has gripped him now. I am not strong
enough, his fears keep bleating out
to fight this fight, this deadly bout.
Yes, *deadly* is the only word.
Dead he will be when I have heard
confession pouring from his lips.
Or me, I'll be as good as dead
if this is all just in my head.
A puddle dodged. Again fear grips.
Can I be right that down below
a sex-fiend lies beneath the show?

A puddle missed. A muddy shower
leaves legs and shoes a dirty mess.
Jack wants to turn, to go and scour
away that mud. He feels unless
when Guthrie sees him he looks smart
he'll come off worst and then depart
his tail betwen his legs. Or so
he tries to tell himself. But, no.
He knows that that's a poor excuse
to put the hour of no-return
one minute back, and so to earn
those seconds free of sharp abuse.
Or, worse, a minute hearing him
tear himself, yes, limb from limb.

But something in him onward drives.
He knows it's there. He feels it there,
although he would not for nine lives
put name to it. Oh no, he'd swear
if you said *British pluck*, or said
Duty's call or *It was bred
in you: the side I never will
let down*, you're wrong. But to instil
such virtues – which is what they are –
has been the thrust of all the teaching
he has had. He's scorned as preaching
much of it. But it's his star,
however little he is able
to lay such cards down on the table.

So this he'll bring to any battle.
But, once again, he tries to feel
that his case is tittle-tattle.
Then knows it's not. Oh no, Jack Steele,
no getting past it: F.H.R.
is guilty, and I know there are
no circumstances that will alter
anything at all. I palter
if I pretend it is not so.
But now – admit one error more:
it was not really me who saw
Guthrie's guilt. No, now I know
Bulaki put the thought in me.
If there's a hero, yes, it's he.

A revelation on the road
to Tarsus. Or the Hospital.
Jack feels the lifting of a load.
Or one laid on? Yes, put a little   He does not
weight in either scale, it is   know whether
the same, whichever pan. Not his   this does him
the mind that worked. No, subtly guided,   good or not.
he sees however much he's prided
himself as bit by bit he saw
the case build up, it was not him.
He knows it now. Oh God, how dim
I've been. But now I can't ignore
the truth. The case began to crack
as soon as he said, 'Sahib, the jack.'

At last the Hospital looms up.
How will I find him now, he thinks.
Delirious? Dead? Well then the cup
will not be there for he who drinks.
But if he's better? Lying there,
exhausted, calm, the ward quite bare,
the *punkah wallah* there outside
tugging his rope, him wide-eyed
staring at the flapping cloth,
what then? The thoughts there in his head?
I have done murder and the dread
of what may follow? Burnt-wing moth
fearing the sharp descending hand
that blots out all? Is he unmanned?

Unmanned, the man who was a man?
Guthrie, my guide, a wandering soul?
Wishing perhaps his pupil can,
despite his lack, reach to the goal?
Or wanting life, wanting to dodge
the waiting fate, to somehow bodge
pursuit? First wanting one and then
the other? Or – let's think again –
could it be that he, now better,
is waiting till he's wholly fit
to come back and do his bit
to keep the law right to the letter
in this his given Indian patch?
And thinking: was Steele up to scratch?

And now inside and Matron greeted
(Doctor Prosser turns away),
now I must ask: is he still heated?
Still do fever's coils hold sway?
'Good news,' the Matron, chirpy, beams
– who would have thought in wildest dreams
that she had heard that stream of dirt? –
'You can take it for a cert
he'll be about tomorrow, or
at worst next day.' Jack tries a smile,
but under it and all the while
his heart is leaden, to the core.
In just a minute, even less,
he must ask Guthrie to confess.

He finds him lying, as he guessed,
listless, drawn, paper-pale.
But not, Jack thinks, too much distressed.
So nothing now to stop the tale
he's got to get this man to tell.
Oh why, oh why, is he now well?
'Good morning, sir, I see you're better.'
Not this the way that I will get a
guilty word from F.H.R.
He's tough, chockful of British grit.
Soft soap is not the way of it.
'Sir, some questions still there are
in my mind, and I must hear
your answers. Answers loud and clear.'

At once in Guthrie's eyes he saw
one answer, one he fully dreaded.
Guilt written there. And something more?
Relief? Yes, that. The two were wedded.
And now he smiles, a pallid smile
but yet a smile. Rueful. Guile
all gone, if ever it had been.
Instead a questing look of keen
curiosity. 'Well, now,
where is that trusted formula
you have been taught, the regular
arrest? Have you forgotten how?
Well, my boy, no need to fret.
I'll take the decent way-out yet.'

'Sir, shoot yourself? That was the way
you hinted once a white man should
if he was found, well, *in flagrante*
take a gun, and if he could
end it in a decent manner.
Four *pais*, they say, to every *anna*.'
'Well, yes, my boy. But with a gun
goes gup. A shot and it's begun,
the rumour mill, its clack, clack, clack.
I know a better way to fall.
Jack Prosser has the wherewithal.'
Jack heard in that, the one word *Jack*.
'But – But –' he said. 'You made me ask
all round for Jack, godawful task.'

Guthrie grinned, a weakish grin.
'Yes,' he answered, 'I thought Jack-
hunting might keep you within
bounds. Or well off my track,
should you ever realise
No, Jack, no was in your eyes
not yelled in fear but at a card
Milly found that some blackguard
had not counted in her pack.
But, well, you were too good for me.
You worked out that it had to be
not any manjack but a jack
of diamonds, spades or clubs or hearts.
It seems that you're a lad of parts.'

Jack could have given credit then
where it belonged, Bulaki Ram.
But – sudden shaft of acumen –
at once he knew that that would harm
that clever chap, after all, a black,
one who should never get a crack
at problems of the masters' weight.
But, worse than harm, it was Ram's fate,
Jack dimly saw, always to strive
to stay in shadow. Though not sure
quite why this was, he knew no cure
was there in 1935.
He felt that soon he'd see the light,
if now it all was dark as night.

So the answer that he gave
to Guthrie's unexpressed request
was with mock modesty to waive
claim to Sherlockian bequest.
'Oh well, it just occurred to me.
I'm sorry that it had to be.'
A silence fell. So what comes next,
Jack thought. His mental muscles flexed.
And then, while in the little ward,
only the punkah's flap was heard,
in his head a something stirred
– the famous organist's lost chord –
hint of a truth he almost held.
Only to find it then disspelled.

'Now, lad, I think that we have done.
Time to take my medicine.
Good God, I think I've made a pun,
but never mind. You'll find it in
that cup and saucer over there.
Prosser measured it with care,
enough at once to put me out.
One swig, and, yes, the law I'll flout.'
He grinned at that. But Jack's aghast.
'Funny, me, the law-enforcer ...
Prosser used the cup and saucer
to hide our trick up to the last.
Right, lad, would you be so good
as to be *Mother*, if you would.'

Would you be so good, Jack thinks.
There's irony as sharp as sharp.
Is it good? Or, it plain stinks?
Do I obey? Or do I carp?
He goes and takes the fatal cup.
Pass it across, or tip it up?
Cost what it may, bring truth to light?
Or, connive, a two-faced knight,
in making this his suicide
look like a natural-causes death?
Arrange it all so not a breath
of scandal's here? Conceal it, hide?
Hypocrisy. Yes, at its worst.
With that mean crime I'm to be cursed?

'Oh, come on, Jack, just give it here.
You cannot make a fellow wait
when he's rejected his last fear,
made up his mind, accepted Fate.'
Then Jack knows it's what he'll do.
Guthrie's a man it's easy to
admire. A man like one his aim
has been to be himself. Not fame
to strive for. But to be, not seem.
To do what's right and stick to that.
To play the game, a good straight bat.
Yes, Guthrie fell. But had his dream.
With steady step Jack goes across.
Cup seized, drunk in a single toss.

A funeral. The grave once more
that in the heat too soon awaits.
The funeral that Jack before
had, in his mind's eye, thought the Fates
would bring him as he by the bed
looked down at Guthrie, thought half-dead.
But here's a change, a change that he
could not in his worst dream foresee.
In the pulpit now he stands,
ordered there by Mr Wright.
'I think you, Steele – it's only right –
should pay a tribute. In your hands
just what to say. I know that you
will speak in words both sad and true.'

What did he mean, poor Jack had thought.
Can it be he somehow knows
what happened when back there I caught
the six-hit ball that Guthrie chose
to wham at me? The poison draft
he'd begged to have? That with such craft
Doctor Prosser, drunk or not,
had conspired to see he got?
Did Prosser then behind his hand
whisper the truth? And Mr Wright?
Did he in turn, ever the White
Man, decree with words too bland
that Milly's death should be forgotten?
Was that wisdom? Was it rotten?

And I? My soul I search
but in the end I just agree.
And as I stand here in the church
I am about to say what he
expects me to. To stand and praise
one who, I know, for all the days
that he did right, did wrong at last.
Committed murder, an outcast
from the muster of the good.
Jack looks down at the congregation.
Can I yet find some mitigation
for what he did? Well, if I could
I would. But, no. No, no excuse.
A crime like his deserved the noose.

He launches out. The words then come.
Not quite those that in the night
he had prepared, a kettledrum
of praises, this and that, left and right,
a ragbag of just what he guessed
Mr Wright would like expressed.
But, no. Here within God's church
he finds a hymn without a smirch
to the man who should have gone
wherever Guthrie used to go.
An image. Then he starts to know
that that is right, and thereupon
he brings his discourse to an end
with not a word that could offend.

Yes. Yes, he thinks. Yes, now I know.
Hypocrisy is not all bad.
Some – our life decrees it so –
with clothes of power are duly clad.
Chance it is that gives them those.
Not virtue, it's not what they chose.
It chose them. But, once so dressed,
brief authority at best,
those trappings they must always flaunt.
Unless they do – and *they* is me –
their lack of clothes the child will see.
The underlings will turn and taunt
us with our lack of proper power.
And we must have our little hour.

**What he almost
grasped before
he now sees
with clarity.**

Someone must rule or there will be
chaos for whatever land
is left to wander lost and free.
We all require a guiding hand
to arbitrate between, say, two
parties with the right to do
whatever they want to have done
when there is room for only one.
So hypocrites there have to be,
the rulers with their tinsel crown.
But this you learn (or else you drown):
at every instant you must see
yourself as posing in the glass.
Fail there, and then your role's a farce.

And this is why – a sudden light –
I never could have joined my life
to Jessica's. She was too bright.
Or not quite bright enough. My wife,
if ever I possess one such,
must either know, yes, just as much
as I've just learnt, or know much less.
Either know, or never guess
what lies behind the brave display.
So when Jess is leaving here,
tonight, tomorrow, I will bear
to see her going on her way.
Meanwhile, and this for many a day,
I'll play the White Man. But I'll play.

Jack Steele, a boy a week ago,
is now a man. Thus do we grow.

GLOSSARY

Aleem-din Hamir: ancient Urdu poet
Angrezland: *angrez* is a common Indian version of 'English'
anna: Indian coin current in 1930s, a sixteenth of a rupee

Ballantyne: R.M. Ballantyne (1825–94), writer of stories for boys
bearer: Indian servant
bolo: speak (imperative form in Hindi)
brain-fever bird: common Indian bird with a very monotonous call
burra: large (in Hindustani); hence *burra peg*, 'a large drink', and
    burra sahib, 'a great man'

charpoy: from the Hindi *charpai*, a bed
chhokra: boy (in Hindi)
chhota hazari: small meal (in Hindi), i.e. a pre-breakfast snack
chillicracker: abusive term formerly used in India for a person of
    mixed race
compound: fenced or walled-in area with a group of buildings
cousin-brother: translation of an Indian term mingling cousinship and
    the male sibling

D.C.: District Commissioner
D.S.P.: District Superintendent of Police
dacoit: robber
daftar: office
did-you-do-it: English for a common Indian bird, based on its call
dine dirty: Raj expression for not wearing evening dress for dinner
Drawing Room: reception held by the British monarch

ek: one (in Hindi)
ek dum: at once (in Hindi)
ekka: one-horse open carriage

First XI: senior team of eleven cricket players
four-pound note: banknote that never existed, hence a fake

gup: gossip, rumour

hathi: elephant
Henty: George Alfred Henty (1832–92), writer of adventure yarns for
    boys, notably *With Roberts to Kabul*

jee: yes (in Hindi)
John T: John Thomas, one of many terms for the penis
Jubilee: twenty-fifth anniversary in 1935 of King George V's
    accession to the throne, his silver jubilee

Kali: Indian goddess of destruction; *The Swashbuckler and the Evil Kali* is a fictitious film to be found in H.R.F. Keating's *The Sheriff of Bombay*

King-Emperor: title assumed by Queen Victoria and inherited by her heirs until the British Empire became the Commonwealth

Kya-naam: literally 'What name', i.e. What's-his-name

marriage plans: in the 1930s junior officers in the Indian police were forbidden to marry until a certain rank and pay was reached

memsahib: lady, usually British, sometimes referred to as a *mem*

mounting block: square stone used to assist a rider mount a horse

musth: on heat (of elephants)

Mutiny: Indian Mutiny of 1857–59, now known in India as the First War of Independence

nimbu pani: lemonade

pai: smallest coin in India; four to the anna in the 1930s

plum duff: suet pudding stuffed with prunes; hence the nickname for anyone called Duff

poodle-faker: now out-dated expression for a man, usually an officer, who for the time being rather than habitually cultivates the society of women

Punjab: region in north-west India

punkah: fan, often of cloth suspended from the ceiling and worked by a *punkah wallah* posted outside to pull a rope rhythmically

quod: prison (British slang)

raja: king, including the playing card (in Hindi)

rani: queen

Rudyard's honest serving men: reference to Kipling's poem on the usefulness in writing of such words as *where*, *who* and *when*

sadhu: wandering holy beggar

sahib: used after a name in Hindi to mean 'Mister'; in English (pronounced sa'ab), used as a synonym for 'gentleman'

Sam Browne: military-style leather belt with a strap over the shoulder, invented by General Sir Sam Browne V.C. (1824–1901), a veteran of the Indian Mutiny

six-hit: cricket term, of a ball hit for the equivalent of six runs

Station: British post in India

tash ka gulam: Hindi expression for the knave or jack at cards

Tell no lies you are not in court: a nicely cynical Indian saying

thik hai: Hindi equivalent of 'okay'

topee: sun-hat with a lining of light sola pith

whisky *pani*: whisky and water, or whisky and soda